PRAISE FOR IRIS MORLAND

He Loves Me, He Loves Me Not

A hilarious, sexy and heartwarming romantic comedy...you do not want to miss this fun, feel-good romance.

— MARY DUBÉ, CONTEMPORARILY EVER AFTER

...refreshing, funny, emotionally charged, and very entertaining to read.

— CAROL, TIL THE LAST PAGE

There is humor, there is heart and there is heat in this story! I absolutely loved it! . . . Mari and Liam delivered. Yowza, their chemistry was palpable.

— BIBLIOPHILE CHLOE

Petal Plucker

Funny, charming, and utterly captivating! I devoured this sparkling read.

— ANNIKA MARTIN, NEW YORK TIMES
BESTSELLING AUTHOR

Petal Plucker was funny, entertaining, fresh and fan-yourself-worthy . . . Their enemies-to-lovers romance is both charming, tender and steamy, and you'll love both of these characters (and their families!) and their sigh-worthy happily ever after.

— MARY DUBÉ, CONTEMPORARILY EVER AFTER

Morland has created a masterpiece of a romance . . . one of my favorite [books] of the year.

— CRISTIINA READS

Humorous, raunchy, and refreshing, Petal Plucker has rightfully earned its way, in my opinion, as one of the best romantic comedy [books] this year.

— CAROL, TIL THE LAST PAGE

My One and Only

This book was gripping, well written & the chemistry between the characters sizzled throughout this wonderful read.

— AMAZON REVIEW

All I Want Is You

Another heartfelt, steamy, terrific story. This is an author who really knows how to create a story that catches a reader's attention and characters that capture her heart.

— BOOKADDICT

TAKING A CHANCE ON LOVE

Thea and Anthony are in for a surprise when it comes to the language of the heart . . . I am in awe.

— HOPELESS ROMANTIC BLOG

Then Came You

This story really pulled all my heartstrings. This was truly a beautiful story and makes you believe there really is true love out there.

— MEME CHANELL BOOK CORNER

ALL I ASK OF YOU

HERON'S LANDING

IRIS MORLAND

BLUE VIOLET PRESS LLC

All I Ask of You (Heron's Landing Book 2)
Published by Blue Violet Press LLC
Seattle, Washington

Published 2020.

First edition published 2016 under the title Tempt Me Tenderly (Heron's Landing Book 2). Second edition 2020.

For all of my author friends.

AUTHOR'S NOTE

Dear Readers,

Before you begin Jaime and Grace's story, please know that *All I Ask of You* was previously published under the title *Tempt Me Tenderly*. This second edition has been lightly edited and changed to better fit the overall feel of the rest of my catalogue.

All my best,
Iris

ALL I ASK OF YOU

When Grace Danvers saw Jaime Martínez for the first time since he'd rejected her advances, she almost fell out of a window.

Before her near defenestration, Grace had been having a fairly good day. It was lovely and warm for November, as two days prior it had been in the thirties, while now it was edging into the upper sixties by mid-morning. Grace had forced herself to go to the vineyard, River's Bend, that morning to drop off a cell phone charger for her brother Adam, who was the vineyard's owner. River's Bend had just hosted its first wedding and was currently working to expand into events after it was hit with three bad years of harvest.

That wedding had also been the place Grace had thrown caution to the wind and had told Jaime about her feelings for him.

She winced thinking about it, standing in the open waiting room at River's Bend. After telling Kerry, the front desk woman and Adam's assistant, that she was here, Grace waited for her brother to come see her, as she also needed to talk to him about attending family dinner that evening. She could go back to his office to see if he were in, but Adam's fiancée Joy McGuire tended to lurk there, and Grace had no intention of barging in on them doing…things. Just recently engaged, the two of them had a tendency to exhibit more PDA than any sister wanted to see.

So Grace waited. She stared out one of the windows. The screens were currently gone, as Adam wanted to replace a number of them after summer had ended. She was glad of his timing, otherwise she'd be standing in a swarm of mosquitoes. Grace inhaled the fresh air, trying not to dwell on who else was here at River's Bend right this second—like Jaime.

Jaime Martínez: River's Bend executive chef and the most beautifully striking man in the history of the universe. Well, at least to Grace. When she'd been eighteen years old, newly arrived Jaime had let her share his umbrella when a summer storm had suddenly moved in, walking with her to her house. It was only after they'd arrived that she'd realized he'd gotten soaking wet while she'd stayed dry under his umbrella. But he'd just grinned and had said goodbye on her front porch, his dark hair plastered to his head as he had gone back out into the storm.

She'd loved him ever since.

For five years, she'd loved him from afar. Until the wedding, when she'd ruined all of it by asking him to kiss her. He'd told her that he wasn't the man for her and had walked off. After that, Grace had avoided Jaime as best as she could.

"Grace."

She froze. She was turned away from the source of the voice, and she wondered—rather wildly—if she could act like she hadn't heard. But then she heard the person step toward her, and she knew the reckoning had come.

Turning, she looked at Jaime for the first time in a week, and her heart almost burst from her chest. He wore his usual jeans and t-shirt with an apron tied around his waist, although unlike his sous chefs, few stains marred the bright white. His hair had grown overlong, and the ends curled slightly. His eyes, dark and usually full of mischief, were now looking at her with an expression of discomfort that filled her with guilt.

"Your brother wanted me to tell you he was out giving a tour but will be here soon. Or you can give me whatever it is you brought for him." Jaime sounded normal, except for when he'd said "your brother." His voice had grated on the phrase, like it was painful to pronounce.

Grace stepped backward. She couldn't speak; her throat closed. She opened her mouth, but nothing came out.

Jaime stepped toward her, and she stepped back. She didn't even realize she was doing it.

"Are you okay?" he asked, his voice quiet.

She almost laughed. *No, my heart's broken and I'm an idiot, but what's new?* She wanted to tell him that seeing him made her want to crawl into a hole and die. She wanted to apologize. She wanted to go back in time and tell that Grace to keep her mouth shut.

She stepped back. Then back again. And then she realized too late that her heel had hit the wall, and she was pitching backward, falling through the open window into some shrubbery below.

But she didn't fall into the shrubbery. Jaime moved with more speed than she thought possible, and then his arm was around her waist, keeping her from tumbling headlong out the window.

He hadn't let her go yet—that was the first thing she noticed. The second thing she noticed was how warm his arm was around her waist. And the third thing was that he gazed at her with such naked longing that her skin prickled.

Her voice finally returned. She whispered, "I've wanted to tell you. I just, I'm…"

His gaze roved over her face. She could feel his fist clenching against her back. He opened his mouth to speak—

"Jaime," Adam asked as he approached them, "why exactly are you holding my sister out a window?"

Grace squeaked. Jaime yanked her upward and then let go, so quickly that Grace felt dizzy. Had he almost kissed her? But now he wouldn't even look at her, so was that just some kind of fluke?

Then she realized they hadn't responded to Adam's question. Her brother stood, his arms crossed, looking at them suspiciously.

"I almost fell out of the window," Grace blurted. At Adam's eyebrow raise, she explained, "I wasn't paying attention and tripped. Jaime kept me from falling, that's all."

Jaime stuffed his hands into his pockets. "Yep, I didn't want her falling into some prickle bush."

"Uh huh," Adam said. He kept glancing back and forth between the pair, and Grace could feel a blush climbing up her cheeks. Did he know that she'd thrown herself at Jaime? Her blush grew brighter. She couldn't look at Jaime. She was sure her guilt was written all over her face.

"Well, I'm going back to my office. Jaime, could you give

me the next week's menu whenever you get a chance?" Adam uncrossed his arms, but he still kept watching them.

"Sure, I'll get it to you within the hour."

If Grace didn't know any better, she'd say that Jaime's voice was forced. If she strained her own eyes, she could make out how stiff his shoulders were and how he looked like he'd rather be anywhere else than in front of his boss and friend, Adam Danvers.

"Okay...I'll see you two later. Be careful, Grace."

As Adam left them alone, Grace let out a soft sigh of relief. She really, really, really didn't want her older brother to know she'd confessed her feelings to his executive chef.

"I need to get to work." Jaime didn't even give her a chance to respond before stalking off to the kitchen. Grace watched him, his shoulders still stiff, his hands in his pockets, and all she could think about was how dark his eyes had gotten when she'd told him how she felt.

Guilt coiled in her gut, along with the desire and the emotions and the love that made Grace Danvers's inner life more interesting than her outward life. Jaime obviously wasn't happy about what had happened between them, and she'd instigated it.

Grace hated when people were upset with her; her family called her the queen of apologies, even when an apology wasn't necessarily warranted. But she had a feeling she needed to apologize this time because she made things uncomfortable between them. Jaime wouldn't be feeling so awkward if she'd kept silent.

She followed Jaime into the kitchen, where his sous chef, Eric O'Neill, worked alongside him. A few other younger chefs, including some interns, bustled about the kitchen, chopping carrots and cracking eggs and trying to avoid Jaime's wrath if they dared to cut the carrots julienne instead of diced.

Jaime had created a reputation for himself as exacting and rather ruthless, but no one could say that he hadn't also created a restaurant that happened to be a jewel in the middle of nowhere Missouri. When he'd first come on, the restaurant had been little more than a café. Now it was a four-star restaurant with reviews being published in international magazines and blogs, with government officials, celebrities, and other notable figures coming to sample the food.

"Eric!" Jaime picked up a plate of chicken with asparagus spears and polenta. "Did you look at this chicken? This is definitely not cooked through."

Eric, a rather short, bland kind of man in his mid-twenties, made a mulish expression and continued chopping onions. "Yeah, I checked it. It's done."

Jaime just stared at him. Then he set the plate on top of Eric's cutting board with a thump and snatched his knife. He cut into the chicken, revealing a pink center.

Grace winced.

"Does that look done to you? No? Then do it again, and do it right. You're my sous chef, not some kid still in school. I expect you to do better." Jaime waited for Eric to respond, but his sous chef just made another face and then nodded tightly.

Everyone else in the kitchen was staring, but when Jaime looked up, they all scurried to finish their tasks. Grace almost wanted to pick up a knife and begin chopping, just to avoid Jaime's wrath.

She'd been around River's Bend and Jaime long enough to know that although he was a perfectionist, he was also fair.

He'd been patient with Eric in the beginning, but that patience was running thin with the constant mistakes and, she had a feeling, pure laziness. But Adam had told Jaime he couldn't fire *another* sous chef, so he'd stuck it out.

Grace wasn't sure if Eric would make it to the New Year.

Jaime still hadn't noticed Grace, and she watched as he walked back into the pantry. No one else paid attention to her —she blended in fairly easily and was just known as the boss's little sister—so she followed him into the back.

The pantry, brimming with cans and bags of ingredients, was organized and spotlessly clean. Grace had to admire how everything was stacked according to type of ingredient, with nothing in the wrong place. When Jaime had first come to River's Bend, the previous executive chef hadn't cared what the pantry had looked like, and more than once an infestation of cockroaches had resulted.

As Jaime looked for a can of something, Grace cleared her throat. He glanced up, his dark eyes widening.

"Grace."

Her throat closed up, and her heart was pounding so fast she saw stars. It wasn't helpful that Jaime was so *handsome*. That dark hair and those dark eyes and the way he picked up a knife and could chop anything within seconds and how he brushed sweat from his brow and how he rolled his r's ever so slightly—not enough that most people noticed. But Grace noticed.

She noticed everything about him.

She cleared her throat. "I wanted to tell you that I'm sorry." Her voice was rather high, like a squeaky mouse, and she blushed at the sound of it. "I'm sorry if I put you in an awkward position." When he didn't reply, she added, rambling somewhat, "Like if I made you feel uncomfortable, or if I did something you didn't want, because I'd hate to think I did that at all. I wasn't necessarily thinking as clearly that night as I should've been, although that's no excuse, I know that. I just… wanted you to know."

Jaime stared at her, and Grace began fiddling with her braid. It was a compulsive gesture, and if she could pull the elastic out of her braid and redo it, she would, just to give herself something to do. Instead, she pulled on the ends until she knew she was making them more ragged as a result.

Jaime glanced upward, stuffing his hands back into his pockets. "You don't need to apologize," he said gruffly. "You were honest, and that's to be commended."

That wasn't particularly comforting, but at least he wasn't mad, Grace thought.

"But I did want to tell you," he continued, "that I meant what I said: nothing can happen between us." His darkened gaze met hers, and he said in a voice that made her heart stop, "Us together… It would be a disaster. You know that, right?"

Grace almost laughed, because it would be easier than crying. The hilarious thing was that she'd come here to say the exact same thing: she'd been wrong to say anything, to put him in this position. But hearing Jaime say out loud that they'd be a *disaster*? It pierced her clean through. She'd thought, she'd hoped…but no. She should've known.

Don't be naïve, Grace. Did you really think he'd change his mind?

Her mouth trembled. She tried to smile, but she had a feeling it came off as lopsided. The lip tremble always precipitated tears. Biting her cheek, she pulled herself together long enough to say, "Okay, then we're on the same page. We'll act like I didn't say anything." Her voice caught, and she had to stop talking.

Jaime looked at her, as if he knew she was struggling not to cry. He took a hand out of his pocket. But he didn't reach for her. Instead, he shrugged and said, "I need to get back to work."

Grace walked home, hands around herself, letting the tears fall freely and telling herself this was the last time she'd cry over Jaime. She felt stupid, childish, and hurt, and because her mind enjoyed being cruel, she relived how handsome he'd looked in the morning light until she felt bruised inside.

As she approached her parents' house and her childhood home, she wiped her face with quick movements and hoped against hope she could get upstairs to her room before anyone noticed. At the very least, she could say it had been colder than she had anticipated and, in a hurry to get home, she'd gotten rather flushed.

The Danvers' home was a two-story bungalow with a wrap-around porch that had been built in the 1930s. Although they'd since installed central heat and air, it still tended to get drafty in the winter and sticky in the summers. Grace's mom Julia had had the shutters painted blue to go along with the taupe paint, and a few petunias still bloomed in pots out front due to the rather warm November weather. Grace heard a few birdcalls in the nearby trees as she stepped inside the house, the hardwood floor creaking underneath her feet.

She hoped her parents were out on the porch out back, but as luck would have it, her mom stepped into the kitchen and saw Grace the second she stepped inside.

"Oh good, you're back," Julia said, going into the bright

kitchen to pour a glass of lemonade. "Did you give Adam the cell phone charger?"

Grace's shoulders slumped, feeling the charger in her back pocket. "No, I forgot," she said, wincing. "Sorry about that."

"You went all the way out to the vineyard but still forgot? Did you tell him about dinner tonight?" At Grace's headshake, Julia sighed. "What a space cadet you are. Sometimes I worry about you." She placed the pitcher of lemonade back into the fridge. Dressed in a pale pink blouse with dark trousers, Grace's mom looked like she'd stepped out of a J-Crew catalog, even though she didn't work and stayed at home most days. But Julia Danvers never eschewed style, and Grace couldn't remember if she'd ever seen her mom in something as sloppy as pants with an elastic waist.

Grace sat down at the dining room table. Her head hurt. Her heart hurt. Julia sat down across from her, sipping her lemonade.

"Everything okay?" Julia asked, her voice soft.

Grace was tempted to spill everything to her mom, but how could she admit that she'd told Jaime how she felt and now he wanted nothing to do with her? Talk about humiliating. So she got up, got a glass of lemonade, and said with a shrug, "I'm just tired. I think I'm going to take a nap before my shift tonight."

Julia cupped her glass in her hands, saying nothing.

Grace was about to go upstairs when her mom said, "You'll tell me, won't you, if anything's wrong?"

Grace wasn't a good liar. So she didn't look at her mom when she replied, "Of course I will."

Upstairs, she gazed out her window, sipping the tart lemonade. She glanced at her art supplies in the corner, a blank canvas sitting on its easel. After attending the University of Missouri and graduating with a degree in studio art, Grace had returned home, unsure of how to proceed. She'd loved painting since she was a young girl and had even won a number of awards for her work. But after graduation, she'd found herself burnt out and unable to paint a thing. Not to mention, there were few jobs out there for painters.

Suddenly determined to do something, she set her glass on a side table and sat down on the wooden stool in front of her easel, setting up her paints and beginning to mix some colors. She tended to paint abstract paintings, with layers of color and emotions bleeding from the pictures like tears on a page. Swirling the yellow paint, she began lightly creating strokes across the canvas, not even sure what she wanted to paint. She just wanted to see if anything resulted.

Grace layered orange and red and then blue, a blur of colors manifesting on the canvas. It seemed startlingly bright in the dim room, and after a couple of hours had passed, she stood back to examine her work.

It looked…lifeless. Uninspired. It wasn't even a painting of a particular figure or scene: just colors. Smeared, pointless colors. She hated it on sight. Tossing her brush onto a table, she flipped the canvas around so she wouldn't have to look at it. She wondered if her parents would freak out if she started a fire in the fireplace to burn it.

Instead, she got ready for work and made sure to scrub the paint from her fingers until they ached.

CHAPTER TWO

When Jaime found Eric outside smoking instead of prepping for tonight's dinner, he had to restrain himself from kicking his sous chef in the shins and send him packing.

To be fair, he wasn't in the best of moods. He hadn't been the moment he'd seen Grace in River's Bend's front room, looking like some kind of angel out to haunt him—did angels haunt people?—with all of that long, blonde hair and light eyes. She had the creamiest complexion with freckles dotting her nose, and he was pretty sure even her eyelashes were tipped with blonde. Add to that a swan's neck, a rosebud mouth, a sweet smile...

Jaime groaned. He couldn't do this. He couldn't lust after his boss's younger sister who also happened to be seven years his junior. What kind of asshole did that make him? And now he'd definitely hurt her when he told her they'd be a disaster together.

Standing outside, he shaded his eyes, taking a deep breath.

He couldn't take his frustration out on Eric—even if the lazy asshole deserved it—and he couldn't take it out on his staff, either. They didn't know he'd effectively cockblocked himself and was dealing with the consequences. Maybe he just needed to get laid.

It had been six months, but who was there to date in tiny Heron's Landing? The pickings were slim in terms of single, eligible women, and Jaime had already slept with two of them (which seemed excessive, given how small the population already was). He didn't want to expand that list any further.

Thus, his current torment. He told himself he just wanted sex. He refused to think that he could just want Grace Danvers. She was like a younger sister to him: he'd known her since she was eighteen years old, for Christ's sake. She's been starry-eyed and hopeful for the future, just about to attend college and do all of the things you're supposed to do when you're in your early twenties.

Jaime envied Grace that, in a way. His parents had emigrated from El Salvador to Missouri with next to nothing except a job offer from Washington University in St. Louis for his dad, Fernando.

An archeologist specializing in Mayan culture, Fernando had worked at the university for close to three decades now, while Jaime's mother Ana had owned her own jewelry store— now expanded to two more locations—for just as long. They were the embodiment of the American dream. Jaime had been born—a surprise to both of his parents—five years after their arrival in the States.

Jaime had worked his entire life: in his mother's store and then culinary school. He didn't regret his path, but sometimes he wondered what life would've been like if he could've just gone to school, figured things out, and maybe relaxed for once.

Relaxing is for rich people, he thought wryly.

Jaime saw that Eric was finishing off his cigarette, dropping it onto the ground without a backward glance. Jaime gritted his teeth.

He'd gone through three sous chefs this year, and Adam had forbidden him from firing Eric preemptively. At his interview, he'd seemed capable. But after Eric had realized he couldn't coast, he'd become sullen and lazy, probably because he knew that even if he were fired, he'd just find another position without hurting for money. His parents were loaded—his dad was a senator, for Christ's sake—and would pay his rent if he asked them.

Jaime had nothing against with people who made more money than him—that was life, and he was happy with his life as it was now. But guys like Eric who thought they were too good to work hard, who had had everything paid for and had never had to face consequences for bad decisions? Yeah, Jaime wasn't a huge fan of people like Eric.

But Jaime wouldn't dwell on that mess right now. He waited until Eric returned inside before following him. He got together the menus for next week and remembered that he still needed to talk to Adam.

Adam, who had seen him holding his sister out a window. He winced inwardly. Did he suspect that his executive chef had turned down his sister? If he did, there'd be hell to pay. Not because Adam wanted them together—no way in hell. But making her cry? That would be bad news. Adam had a tendency to see his sister as a little girl in need of his protection, and if he thought Jaime had done anything to hurt her, even unintentionally?

Well, to say Jaime's balls would be ripped from his body would be an understatement.

It doesn't matter, because it's done. I did the right thing. I can't feel guilty about that.

Jaime entered Adam's office, the door unlocked, only to find his boss in an embrace with his fiancée Joy. Joy had bright purple hair that was currently up in some complicated hairstyle, chandelier earrings jingling as she laughed. Adam looked at her like she hung the moon in the sky and caused the earth to rotate on its axis, and if Jaime weren't so uncomfortable watching them, he'd be jealous.

"Oh, Jaime, there you are." Adam didn't let go of Joy, but she turned to Jaime as well. "Do you have the menu ready?"

Jaime watched as Adam stroked Joy's bare arm. He was happy for his friend—he really was. Adam had been so lost after the death of his wife Carolyn that when Joy had entered the picture, everyone had been thankful. Until Adam had screwed things up, but they'd managed to find their happy ending.

Jaime placed the menus on Adam's desk. "Joy, it's nice to see you. Any new stories brewing that will piss off your fiancé?"

Joy laughed. "I've been too busy to write, but there's always something up here." She tapped her temple. "It also helps that it's so easy to rile Adam." Patting his chest, she added, "Isn't that right, honey?"

"I don't know why I put up with you," Adam said.

She smiled. "Do you want me to answer that right now?"

"Behave yourself." Turning back to Jaime, Adam asked, "How's everything going? Is Eric improving?"

Jaime grimaced. "Can I be honest? I'd like to punt kick the kid into the river."

"I think this is my sign to exit." Joy leaned up to kiss Adam on the cheek. "See you later?"

"See you. Try not to do anything I wouldn't do."

Joy just waved a hand as she left.

Going around to his desk, Adam sat down, and Jaime sat down across from him. "What's Eric done now?" Adam asked.

"Well, for one, he can't cook worth a damn. Two, he's lazy. Three, he's a spoiled brat. I could go on, but I'd rather fire him and find someone worthwhile."

"And fire the fourth sous chef we've hired this year? I hate to even say this, but do you ever wonder if it's you that's part of the issue?"

Jaime knew it was him—but that wasn't the problem. He had exacting standards, while all of these boys sat on their asses and thought they didn't have to work hard because mommy and daddy would always take care of them.

But he didn't say any of that. Instead, he said in measured tones, "I know I'm a hard ass. But they aren't going to become great chefs otherwise."

"I get that, and you do amazing work." Adam rubbed his forehead. "We just have too much on our plate right now. Eric isn't my favorite person either, but can you try to work with him? At least until after the New Year? We have four weddings and the farm to table event in April to focus on."

Jaime didn't want to spend one more second coddling Eric

O'Neill, but Adam was still his boss. So he nodded tightly and muttered something about "doing his best."

Adam looked at his monitor and opened up what was probably an email. Scanning what looked like a spreadsheet, Jaime watched as he frowned and made "hmmm" sounds at his computer for a few moments.

"Are you going to share why you're grunting at your computer, or should I leave you two alone?" Jaime asked.

Adam looked up, as if he'd forgotten Jaime was there. "Oh, sorry. It's just a financial spreadsheet sent over from the CPA. These numbers aren't adding up…" He frowned again. "Sam must've put in some numbers wrong. Anyway, that's neither here nor there. What are your thoughts about getting chefs from around the state for this farm to table thing?"

Jaime was glad to talk of something else. He gave Adam a list of potential chefs in the state who could be invited, along with ideas for panels and food served. Ever since the harvest had been abysmal for the past three years, River's Bend had since expanded into events, hosting its first wedding only a week ago. That same wedding where Jaime had rejected his boss's sister even though if he were remotely honest with himself, he'd admit how much he'd wanted to reciprocate.

He shook off the memory. He could not let himself get distracted. He had work to do, a restaurant to run, a boss to keep happy, and a sous chef to avoid murdering. Getting entangled with Grace Danvers would be career suicide.

After talking with Adam, Jaime returned to the kitchen to finish prepping for tonight. This was a slower time of year for the restaurant, and he didn't expect a huge crowd. But that didn't mean he didn't want the food to be perfect each time: it didn't matter if a customer was a state senator or some local from Heron's Landing. Every time they served food, it should be amazing.

Eric, though, seemed hell bent on doing the exact opposite. Jaime caught him texting in the pantry when he should've been prepping. Later, Eric overcooked the salmon, and Jaime almost tossed the plate in his sous chef's face. A headache was threatening, and this was one instance when he wished he were the boss of River's Bend and could fire anyone he wanted.

Technically speaking, he could fire Eric, but Adam had asked him to stick it out. So he would stick it out. Even if it drove him to drink, he would do it, at least until after the New Year. The last thing Jaime wanted to do was add to Adam's plate when the vineyard still wasn't out of the red completely.

As the night wore on, Jaime began muttering in Spanish, calling Eric all kinds of names he wouldn't understand. Everyone knew when Jaime spoke Spanish in the kitchen was when he was pissed. The words flowed in a river of rolled r's and slightly lisped c's, the accent regional to El Salvador and how his parents spoke Spanish at home.

At any rate, by the time he got to go home, Jaime had decided a bottle of wine would be his best partner. Sometimes he hated Heron's Landing—or rather, hated how small and insular it was—while other times it had been the place he'd felt most at home. It was a strange contrast, and one he'd yet to fully reconcile. He had friends here—Adam most of all—but oftentimes he still felt like the strange foreigner, even though he was just as American as his sous chef.

And of course, there was Grace. Grace! In his mind, Jaime had begun calling her Graciela, and sitting on his couch, he leaned his head back and sighed. *Graciela, Graciela, what am I going to do with you?*

When he'd first met her, he had to admit, he'd barely noticed her. She'd been shy, young, her long hair in her face, and she'd stuttered her name and subsequently hadn't said another word when Jaime had come over for dinner at the Danvers' home that first time. Back then, Carolyn had still been alive, and she and Adam had kept the conversation going, laughter and jokes filling the room.

Even the Danvers patriarch and the boss of River's Bend at the time, Carl, had been in a good mood. Jaime had just been offered the job of executive chef at River's Bend, and he had all kinds of ideas of how to bring the restaurant to a whole new level. Although Carl had been skeptical, Adam had been wholly supportive.

Grace, though, hadn't said much during that dinner. She'd just watched, passing a bowl of food whenever asked. Jaime had sat next to her and had tried to engage her in conversation, but she'd been so shy that he'd eventually given up. He'd been twenty-five and too interested in himself to draw out an awkward eighteen-year-old who wore long skirts and bangles.

Something had shifted since then. After Grace had returned to Heron's Landing after receiving her degree in studio art, she'd blossomed. Oh, she looked only a little bit older, and she still wore her hair in braids, but she wasn't that shy girl of eighteen. She was a woman now, and Jaime—goddamn him—had noticed.

Jaime closed his eyes. He'd never, in his wildest dreams, would've thought Grace would approach him and confess her feelings. He'd known she liked him—he'd be an idiot not to notice, but he'd assumed she'd be too shy to say anything to him. When she'd come to him, wearing that dress, her mouth red and her creamy skin glowing in the lamplight? He'd been lost.

"Fucking hell, I'm a mess," he muttered to himself. He took the bottle of wine and stuffed it back into the fridge. He wasn't drunk, but he was buzzed enough that he was becoming sentimental. Since when did he sit at home and cry over a woman he couldn't have? He must be losing his damn mind.

About to turn in for the night, he heard his phone ring. To his surprise, it was Adam. He never called this late. Suddenly worried, he picked up. "What's up?" he asked.

"Sorry to be calling you this late," Adam said. He didn't sound upset, but he did sound stressed. "But you know that financial spreadsheet from earlier?"

Jaime had forgotten all about it. "Yeah, what about it?"

"I looked into it further, and there's evidence that someone is stealing money from the vineyard."

Jaime sat back down. Who would steal from River's Bend? He couldn't believe it. "How do you know? And do you know who it could possibly be? Jesus, Adam, this is the last thing we need." His mind started whirling, trying to figure out what this would mean. They were already in the red enough: losing money like this could be a death sentence.

"It's not absolutely conclusive. But there are traces, traces that Sam sent me. We're going to call a detective tomorrow and launch an investigation." Adam paused, and Jaime could just imagine his friend clenching his jaw.

"But do you know who?" Jaime ran through the people who worked there—Kerry, Adam's assistant; Chris, the groundskeeper; Leah, the wine tasting coordinator. Would any of them do such a thing? He couldn't imagine any of them would.

"That's the thing." Adam took a deep breath. "All of the evidence points to one person—and that person is you, Jaime."

CHAPTER THREE

As Grace grabbed her paint supplies and stalked out of the house, she wished her hands weren't so full that she couldn't slam the front door as well.

Why don't you try to get a real job instead of wasting time down at Trudy's?

What are you going to do with your life?

Her dad's words echoed in her mind, making her stomp down the path that would lead to the river. It wasn't that her dad was wrong, but Grace simply didn't have an answer to his questions. She'd gone to school to paint, she'd earned her degree, she'd tried to find some kind of job that would allow her to continue painting...but she'd quickly realized she'd have to move back home if she didn't want to starve. She'd applied for other kinds of work—office jobs, retail, even a dog walker—but no bites. Grace had a degree with no work experience, and the economy being what it still was, no one wanted to take a chance on a twenty-three-old when they could hire a forty-three-year-old with two decades of experience instead while paying that middle-aged worker half what they deserved.

The weather had finally turned chilly, like fall was supposed to be. The leaves had changed into bright reds, oranges, and yellows, and they crunched underneath Grace's feet as she walked down to the river. It was a spot she'd come to often as a young child, mostly to get away from her annoying older brothers, and now she used it as a place to clear her mind.

She also hoped the gorgeous scenery would inspire her to paint. Even if she painted some hotel lobby landscape, something was better than nothing. She hadn't completed a painting since before graduation.

Grace shivered a little as she sat down on the hard ground, setting up her painting supplies. She had on leggings underneath her skirt and sweater, but the wind had enough bite that she probably should've brought a jacket. But she refused to go back home and face her dad right now. He only criticized her lately, like she could never be good enough in his eyes. He'd never understood why she had wanted to paint, and now that she was working minimum wage and living at home, his arguments that she should've majored in something practical were proving fruitful.

Grace hated that he'd been right, in a way. She would've hated studying business or communications, but she'd have a job, wouldn't she? At least she wouldn't be under her dad's thumb like she was right now.

She sighed. She brushed a few tendrils of her long hair behind her ear, wondering again if she should cut it. She'd had it long for so many years that it felt like another limb. But lately she'd wanted to push the boundaries—even just by cutting her hair—but she'd yet to get the courage to do it. She could hide behind her hair when she needed to, and that was a security she wasn't willing to sacrifice at the moment.

Grace began mixing, focusing on the fiery colors of fall. The river provided a calm backdrop, with some birds calling overhead. The rains of spring had caused the river to rise almost above its banks, but now it was mostly back to normal. Spotting a heron flying down and banking onto the other side, she smiled. Sometimes she would come here to watch for birds, sometimes to fish for crawdads. When she was little, she'd bring a plastic container and search for tadpoles to bring home. Her mom always grimaced when she'd shown her the bowl of tiny amphibians, their tails bustling behind them as they swam in circles.

Grace swirled dark orange paint onto the canvas, attempting to create trees and perhaps the river in front of her. She usually found landscapes uninspired, but now she was determined to paint something. She'd be just like Bob Ross and paint mountains and rivers and *happy little* trees and a stray bird overhead and clouds and everything banal. If she could catch a squirrel and keep it in her pocket like Bob did, she would do that, too.

She painted as the afternoon waned on, creating the river, trying to paint shadows in its corners and currents. She painted a blue-gray sky, a few cirrus clouds swirling around its depths. She even added the heron, its leg uplifted and its beak to the sky. For a few moments, she stopped and watched as it fished, and she laughed out loud when he caught one and gulped it down.

As the sun began to lower in the sky, she could feel the temperature dropping with it. Her once sunny spot had transformed into a shady one, and she couldn't stop shivering. She really should've brought a jacket. At the thought of forgetting important weather gear, she couldn't help but think of when Jaime had let her stand under his umbrella that rainy day so many years ago—the day she'd fallen in love with him.

She'd tried to forget about him. She'd dated other guys in college, but the relationships never lasted beyond a few months. Sometimes Grace wondered if she were broken: the kissing was nice, but eventually she'd get bored and want to go home. Now she was twenty-three and a virgin, and she found it somewhat embarrassing. How'd she get to be a college graduate without losing her V card? Then she felt stupid for feeling stupid, because virginity was a social construct and meant nothing anyway...

Looking at her painting, she realized that it was crap. Absolute, complete, toss-it-into-the-dumpster-right-now crap. It looked like an imitation of a hotel painting that had been traced from a second grader's drawing. Growling and swearing at herself, Grace wished she used paper as a medium so she could tear it up into tiny pieces. But, alas, canvases weren't that easily destroyed, and throwing it into the river would be rude, so she just laid back onto the dirt and huffed out a breath. She threw her arms across her eyes and screamed a little, like a little kid. She was just glad she was alone.

"Grace?"

She shot up so quickly that she knocked over her easel with her foot and sent her paint supplies skittering across the rocky ground. And to make things even better, Jaime himself stood in front of her, looking rumpled and *delicious.* She hated him on sight. He needed to go away already and let her live her life. Dammit, now her paintbrush was soaked in river water and river goop and some of her paint had spilled, too.

Jaime crouched down to help her. "Sorry if I scared you. Were you painting?"

It was a dumb question, and Grace knew that Jaime knew it was a dumb question. But she was too agitated to care. She also didn't want him to see her sad excuse for a Bob Ross landscape painting. "I was trying to," she muttered, tossing her supplies into her bag without looking at them. "But nothing seems to stick."

Jaime glanced at her painting. "That's pretty."

But she could hear in his voice that what he really meant was, *That's boring.* She almost laughed. "It's terrible, and you know it." She finally gave up and sat back, wiping her hands of some of the dirt and eventually giving up.

He sat down beside her. "Well, I wouldn't say it was terrible, but it's not…"

"Interesting? It's okay. It looks like a hotel painting."

Jaime cocked his head, peering at the painting more closely. Then he laughed a little. "It *does* look like a hotel painting. What makes a painting look like a hotel painting, though? Like is there some secret hotel painting store all hotels buy them from?"

"There's probably a shop on Etsy," Grace said dryly.

Jaime laughed again.

Despite herself, she felt her mood lighten somewhat. She'd be a liar if she said she didn't enjoy being in Jaime's company. They hadn't been alone—really alone—since the wedding. Her face burned at the memory. She stared at the ground, but then she caught sight of his hands, and she remembered how they'd felt pressed against her back.

She looked away and forced herself to stare at the river instead.

"Do you come here a lot?" Jaime asked. "I just found this spot recently, but if you've claimed it, I can find another one."

She shrugged. "I've come here since I was little, but it's not like I own this patch of the river."

I also don't want you to leave. I know you've been avoiding me, and I hate it, she thought.

"Well, if you're sure."

After that, silence fell. It wasn't uncomfortable, but Grace wondered if Jaime wanted some time alone. She glanced at him, and she saw that his jaw was tense. He looked tired, and there were circles underneath his dark eyes. Had he not been sleeping? She knew River's Bend needed a lot of work lately, but this seemed different.

She almost asked him what was wrong, but then she thought better of it. She didn't have a right to pry: they weren't even friends, per se, but more like people who ran into each other often. She wrapped her arms around her knees, suddenly feeling the chill again. Maybe she should leave and go home.

"Are you cold? Here, take my jacket."

Jaime shrugged off his jacket and placed it over her shoulders. The jacket was big enough that it was almost like a blanket on top of her, and she inhaled his scent emanating from the cloth. As he placed the jacket on her shoulders, his hands stayed on her upper arms—perhaps longer than necessary.

But then he moved away, and Grace wondered if she'd just been imagining things.

"Thank you," she murmured. She saw that he only wore a

t-shirt now, and she knew how much he hated the cold. "Aren't you going to be cold?"

"I'll be fine. I need to walk back home anyway."

She pulled the jacket closer, her eyes closing. It smelled like spice and cedar and Jaime's warmth seeped into her limbs until she wanted to cry from the exquisite sensation. She wanted to imagine that this was as close to him embracing her as she was going to get, and it broke her heart and made it pound at the same time.

"I guess you're always keeping me safe from the weather," Grace said. When he just looked at her, she blushed. "Never mind," she muttered.

Jaime looked like he wanted to ask what she meant, but he didn't.

She just smiled, her heart cracking a little. She wondered if he even remembered that moment—that moment when he'd smiled at her and held his umbrella over her head while he got soaked to the skin—and she'd fallen in love with him. She wanted to cry at the thought, but it was just too indicative of her life right now: a whole host of small misses that added up until they felt like they were suffocating her.

She heard a phone sound then, and she watched as Jaime took out his phone and then grimaced at what he read. He muttered something in Spanish that sounded like a very complicated and long-winded curse.

Grace couldn't help it. "Is something wrong?" she asked. She probably couldn't do anything to help, but at least it would get her mind off of her own problems.

Jaime looked up at her, as if he'd forgotten she were there. Then he shook his head. "No, just some stupid shit with the vineyard. Actually, it's more complicated than that. Your brother wants to talk to me."

She just stared at him, waiting for him to explain. When he refused to talk, she said quietly, "Anything you say won't go beyond this spot. Not a word to my brother, or anyone else." She held up three fingers. "Scout's honor."

He smiled a little. "I shouldn't tell you this, but then again, you're going to find out anyway. There's money missing from the vineyard."

"What?" Her eyes widened. "Who would steal from River's Bend? It barely has any money to steal right now!"

"Ironic, right? But you haven't heard the best part."

"Is there a best part when someone's stealing money from my family's business?"

"According to your brother, the prime suspect is none other than me."

Grace stared at him. She thought at first he was joking—how could anyone think Jaime would steal from River's Bend? When he'd poured so much of himself into the restaurant? She said nothing, waiting for the "just kidding!", but it never came.

"You're not serious? You? *You?* Has my brother lost his mind?" She got so agitated that Jaime's jacket slipped off, and she was about to get up and find Adam when Jaime put a hand on her arm. That got her to sit back down.

"He doesn't want to believe it, but there's evidence that says otherwise. I guess." He scowled, tossing some rocks into the river. "It's bullshit, of course, but I have to go through the motions anyway, because if I refuse to talk, I'll look guilty, won't I?"

"But how does anyone know it was you? Or think that it could be you?"

He shrugged. "I don't know. Your brother just told me last night, or I guess, warned me. But there's money definitely missing, so they're starting an investigation."

"Whatever happened to innocent until proven guilty?" Grace pulled the jacket closer, clenching her fists until she realized she was probably wrinkling the material. "That doesn't seem fair at all."

"Things aren't fair in this world." He tossed another rock into the river, then sighed. "Sorry, I shouldn't dump my problems onto you, especially when you're connected to it in a way."

"Don't apologize. You should be able to talk about this with someone." In a quiet voice, she added, "I'm glad you feel like you can talk to me."

She ventured to look at him again, and his expression was such a mixture of surprise, resignation, and searching that she didn't know to react. Did he really not have any idea how she felt about him? That it wasn't just some girlish crush? She felt as if he were seeing her for the first time, or just realizing that she was more than Adam's younger sister trying to get a kiss just to pass the time.

His voice low, he said, "I try not to dwell on things I can't do anything about, you know? But I've worked my ass of for this vineyard, and what do I get? Accused of theft. I'd laugh if I weren't so angry about it."

Jaime's voice was so bitter that Grace's heart hurt. She was glad that Adam didn't want to believe his friend was guilty and had seemed to warn him more than accuse him, but at the same time, she couldn't imagine the betrayal Jaime was feeling. To work so hard, only to be investigated for a crime you didn't commit?

She knew he hadn't done it. She didn't need evidence because she knew Jaime Martínez was a good, hard-working, honest man who'd fought tooth and nail to get where he was today. He'd never toss that away—never.

She didn't know what to say, though. She could feel his anger coming off in waves, and she wanted to touch him, to hug him, to tell him it would be all right. They'd figure out who'd done this, or maybe it was just a miscalculation. But those all seemed like hollow platitudes, and none of them were things she could guarantee.

So instead, she said, "I believe you're innocent. For what it's worth."

Jaime looked at her, his gaze dark but seeming to lighten around the edges. She took him in: the stubble on his jaw, his full lips, how he had a slight bump on his nose, how she could make out a few strands of silver on his temples. He wore a necklace with a small, silver cross on it, and she wondered who had given it to him. His mom, or maybe a girlfriend? As long as she'd known him, he'd worn that necklace every day, although she hadn't known him to be particularly religious. There were a lot of things about Jaime that she'd yet to discover, she realized.

She may be in love with him, but she didn't really *know* him.

He swallowed, looking at her. "Thank you. That means a lot to me."

She couldn't hold his gaze. She looked away again, blushing a little, but her heart swelling all the same.

She was in so deep. So deep, and the waters were only

closing in over her head now, drowning her. She'd sink to the bottom without making a sound, and Jaime not being the wiser.

She pulled the jacket closer.

"I should probably get back," Grace said. "It's almost time for dinner anyway."

She was about to get up, but Jaime got up first and then held out a hand. She looked up at him, and she let him envelop her hand with his larger one. Their fingers made a stark contrast—hers pale, his brown—and she had to pull away lest she do something really stupid.

"You have dinner with your parents every night?" he asked.

"Oh, yeah, I guess. I mean, I do live with them."

"That's nice. I miss my mom's cooking. She'd make pupusas de chicharrón every Friday." Jaime made a sound that was a mixture of longing and satisfaction.

"I've never had those," Grace admitted as she began to gather her supplies. Jaime helped her, carrying her easel and ugly painting while she picked up her bag with paints and brush. "What are they? I've heard of them."

"Basically a tortilla stuffed with cheese and pork," he replied. "There's a great place about an hour from here in Belltown that has amazing Salvadorian food. You should take a trip there."

She smiled, but didn't reply. She'd much rather take a trip there with Jaime, or better yet, have him cook for her, but she couldn't really tell him as much.

When they got to the main path, Jaime asked, "I'm in the opposite direction, but do you want me to walk you home? It's getting dark."

"I think the deer and rabbits will leave me be," she said

with a smile, taking her easel and canvas from him. "Thank you, though."

He seemed to be about to say something else, but then just shook his head. He said goodbye, walking off into the distance.

She watched him until he disappeared, a vague figure amongst the shadowy trees. It was only until he was gone that she realized she hadn't returned his jacket. She fingered the cloth, inhaled its scent, and wondered if Jaime would notice if she kept it.

CHAPTER FOUR

J aime had never preferred one kind of woman over the other: green eyes, blue eyes, brown hair, blonde hair. If it was on a woman, he liked it. Tall, short, curvy, thin, brown, white, and everything in between? He'd enjoyed women at his leisure without discrimination.

But now what haunted him was long, blonde hair, like mermaid's hair, falling in soft waves down a pale back. He knew, instantly, who the hair belonged to. Who else could it be? Who else had hair the color of dark wheat that looked amber in the sunlight?

"Graciela." Jaime wrapped an arm around her from behind, smelling her soft hair. It smelled like cherries. He sifted his hands through it, wrapping some of its length around his wrist. He wondered if Grace had ever played Rapunzel as a little girl. *Rapunzel, Rapunzel, let down your beautiful, glorious hair.*

Grace sighed as he kissed the side of her neck.

"Why don't you leave your hair down more often?" It fell

almost to the top of her ass, and he marveled at how long it was and how many colors ran through its strands.

"Do you want me to? Leave my hair down?"

Her voice, a throaty murmur, went straight to his groin. He wanted to wrap his hands in her hair as she rode him, the length covering her breasts, her nipples barely visible. He wanted it splayed across a pillow as he moved insider her from above, her eyes heavy and her mouth parted.

He trailed his index finger up under her cotton shirt. He traced the length of her torso, brushing at the small indentation of her waist. Silk, skin, heat, a small trail of moles, like constellations, across her stomach. Soft hairs dotting the spot above her belly button.

He kissed her neck again, licking, sucking. She breathed harder. He wondered if he could get her to moan—to scream. Or would she be quiet, all in her head?

"Graciela, Graciela," he murmured, saying words in Spanish that he knew she wouldn't understand but that didn't have the right translation in English. They flowed from him like a current, pouring over them, and he could feel her pulse speed up under his tongue. His hand moved upward under her shirt. He cupped her breast—small, warm, the nipple tightened already.

"Do you want me?" he asked.

She pressed her ass against his hardened cock, and it was him who moaned.

"I've wanted you for as long as I can remember." She took his hand, still massaging her breast, and covered it with hers. Squeezed. "Will you take me, Jaime? I want you—I *need* you."

He didn't need to be asked twice.

As he kissed her, open-mouthed and desperate, the sound of a phone going off rang through the room.

And then Jaime opened his eyes, realized he'd been dreaming of Grace Danvers, and that he had a massive hard-on from said dream.

He slapped at his phone, still singing on his nightstand. He glanced down at his crotch, and then he swore.

I'm a fucking creep. The biggest creep. Having sex dreams about my friend's younger sister.

He threw an arm over his eyes, breathing and trying to stop the flow of blood from his head to his cock. But all he could see behind his eyelids was the length of Grace's hair falling down her back, how warm she'd felt, how she'd pressed against him.

Will you take me, Jaime?

"Jesus motherfucking Christ on a cracker!" He tore out of bed, stomping to the bathroom. He splashed cold water on his face. Gazing into the mirror, he muttered, "You need to fucking stop." Then he pointed at his crotch, adding, "And you *really* need to fucking stop! I don't have time for this. This cannot happen."

Dressed just in his boxers despite the cooler weather, he went to the kitchen and began making an omelet. It was early yet, and maybe cooking something would get his mind off of...things. But his mind inevitably returned to that dream, and he burnt one side of the omelet while the other side was still runny. He tossed it all into the trash and decided today was a protein bar and coffee kind of day.

Lots and lots of coffee.

After taking a cold shower, he got dressed and was about to go into work early when his phone rang.

"Hey Dad," he said in Spanish.

"Jaimito, how are you? Your mother and I just wanted to call and tell you we're finishing up our application for citizenship and we had a few questions."

Jaime didn't know if he had the juice for this this morning, but he'd help his parents anyway he could. Both of them spoke English, but the application for citizenship had enough legalese that they preferred to confirm any questions they had with Jaime first.

They had a lawyer, but asking Jaime was just easier in their minds. He couldn't blame them: any kind of mess-up could result in the application being denied, and it was too much time and money not to cross your t's and dot your i's as much as possible.

Fernando rattled off various questions, which Jaime was mostly able to answer, while a few stumped him as well. The US government loved convoluted instructions, and sometimes even Jaime needed Fernando to repeat things to understand what the actual question was.

As they segued into less government-related topics, Fernando turned his phone on speakerphone so Jaime's mother Ana could talk to their son as well. They asked about River's Bend, his job, Heron's Landing, all the usual things.

Jaime winced at their questions, remembering the upcoming investigation—of which he was apparently the center. He couldn't tell his parents about the investigation, especially when he hadn't been charged with anything. It would only worry them. Plus, if Immigration caught wind of it? It could hurt their application.

Jaime knew it was naïve, but he sincerely hoped everything could be pushed under the rug once they figured out that it was either an accounting error or find who had actually stolen the money in the first place.

"Do you still like it there?" Ana asked. She'd been concerned when Jaime had left the big city of St. Louis to go to a tiny Midwestern town like Heron's Landing, population two-hundred and fifty. She'd been afraid Jaime would be lonely, an outsider, not knowing anyone there already.

He glanced at the time. He needed to get to work. "Yeah, it's great. Look, I have to get to work, but email or text me if you have anymore questions about your application, okay?" He grabbed his keys and walked out to his truck.

"Have a good day at work," his parents said in unison. "Love you, Jaimito."

"Love you, too. Talk to you later." He hung up and stuffed his phone in his pocket.

If there was anything he hated, it was not being in control of a situation. He could say he was innocent until he was blue in the face, but what if no one believed him? It didn't matter. It didn't matter what he said or did. It didn't matter how hard he worked, or how talented he was. It didn't matter that he'd transformed River's Bend into the restaurant it was now.

Nothing he did mattered.

I believe you're innocent. For what it's worth.

Grace's words poured through him, a balm to his wounds. She had a sweetness about her, and lightness and, yes, grace, that had intrigued him since he'd first met her five years ago. He hadn't expected she'd go against her brother and support him, but she had. Her declaration wouldn't keep him from facing charges, but someone believed him. Someone knew he was innocent.

The dream from earlier was like a mist over his mind. He

could've almost believed it had been real: the smells, the sounds, the touches. He'd never had a dream like that about Grace Danvers.

Graciela, what am I going to do about you?

When he arrived at River's Bend, the sky was cloudy and he wondered if it would rain. He parked his truck and, going inside, greeted Kerry. He made his way to the kitchen, putting on his apron, and then going to the coffee pot in the corner before starting the day. A few of his cooks were milling about, but generally speaking, they didn't start until Jaime arrived. To his annoyance, Eric was nowhere to be found.

"Coffee ready? Oh, Jaime."

Jaime turned to see Chris, the overseer of the fields and harvesters in the fall, looking at him with a strange expression his face. A middle-aged man, Chris had been at River's Bend back when Adam's father Carl had run it. With his salt-and-pepper hair and skin tanned the color of a walnut, Chris had a distinguished mien. He demanded authority, although he had a soft spot for dogs and his wife (in that order).

"Coffee is almost ready," Jaime replied. "Are you going to be around for lunch?"

River's Bend served lunch on a smaller scale and often that included the employees. But Chris just raised his eyebrows, and then shrugged.

"Not sure I'll have time. Have a lot going on."

Jaime wasn't sure what all he had going on, since this was the time of year when the harvest was already in and nothing was growing. Perhaps Chris had more to do with making the wine than usual? But then again, they usually sent that out to another company to do before receiving bottles of wine to then sell.

"Well, if you want a plate, let me know." Jaime walked around Chris, who didn't seem inclined to move out of the way, to enter into the kitchen. The older man's shoulder bumped into him, and he looked at Chris over his shoulder, a dark eyebrow raised.

But Chris just stared at him, his eyes narrowed. His gray mustache twitched.

"I was surprised, you know, when Carl hired you. I thought you were too young for the job, but he wanted to try someone up and coming. And now here we are."

Jaime bristled. He wasn't so stupid as not to understand what Chris was implying, and God almighty, he wanted to punch the old man in his face. But that would merely but be proving Chris's point.

So instead, Jaime acted nonchalant, a tight smile on his face. "I'm glad Carl gave me a chance. I love this place. I know you do, too."

Chris looked nonplussed at Jaime's non-reaction. Luckily, the coffee pot dinged, breaking the tension.

Jaime motioned to the coffee. "Be my guest."

The day proceeded about as well as the beginning did. Eric showed up an hour late, yawning and laughing about his late night, so Jaime set him on pumpkin prep duty.

Pumpkin prep was the worst, mostly because it involved shaving off the hard rind and then scooping out the mound of squishy pumpkin guts and seeds. But people loved pumpkin-everything around here, and Jaime liked to use it on the fall menu.

"Why don't we just get the canned stuff," Eric muttered, shaking his hand of pumpkin guts and making a disgusted noise.

"Because canned is never as good as fresh. Stop bitching and get to work, or you'll be doing that for the rest of the week."

Eric scowled and proceeded to prep pumpkins as slowly as humanly possible.

Jaime didn't have time for his useless sous chef. He chopped, diced, stirred, sautéed, and baked alongside the rest of his team. He didn't care if Eric bitched and moaned all day long: this was Jaime's kitchen, and if Eric didn't like it, that was his problem.

When lunch rolled around, though, Jaime was about to throw his sous chef out the window. He'd left to go to the bathroom, and thirty minutes later, still wasn't back.

"Aiden, can you go find Eric for me?"

Aiden, a short kid with bright red hair who was interning at River's Bend, said, "Let me finish whipping up these eggs whites…" He kept whipping, wiping sweat from his red forehead with his sleeve.

Jaime tossed his last bit of zucchini into a mixing bowl. "Never mind, I'll do it. Keep whipping, but don't put too much air into them."

"Right-o, boss."

Jaime went to the men's restroom, where he found a grand total of zero Erics. Surprise, surprise. He went to the front desk and asked Kerry if she'd seen him, but she just said as she tapped her chin, "I haven't seen him since this morning. Maybe try out back?"

Jaime squinted at the windows. It was raining, but not much. He didn't really want to go outside and freeze his ass off. But as he walked to the front door, he saw a figure not far away. Jaime wasn't even angry now: just tired. He shouldn't have to pull teeth to get his employee to do basic tasks.

"What are you doing out here?" said Jaime.

Eric was leaning against a wall, smoking a cigarette, hands in his pockets. "Taking a smoke break. What's it look like?"

Jaime glanced at his phone. "You've been on break—without my permission—for over a half hour now. I'd recommend you get back to work or you can pack your things and leave. Your choice."

Eric, though, didn't make a move. Instead, he inhaled on his cigarette, exhaling slowly, the smoke drifting through the haze of light rain.

"I'm not sure you understand what's going on here," Eric said.

Jaime walked up and plucked the cigarette out of his hand, crushing it beneath his shoe. "I'm thinking you're the one who doesn't understand. You have five seconds to get to your job that you were hired for, or you're fired. Is that simple enough for you to understand?"

Jaime knew that Adam would be pissed if he'd fired his fourth sous chef in a year, but he didn't care. Eric could rot: he hadn't added anything positive to his kitchen since the moment he'd arrived.

Eric shrugged. "I'm not sure you have the authority to fire anyone right now. Not when you've been caught stealing money from your boss."

Jaime stilled. His fists clenched, and he almost picked Eric up by his shirt collar and slammed him against the wall. The rain fell a little harder, cold and piercing.

"You don't know what you're talking about. I don't appreciate threats, either. You're one step away from being fired."

"You can't fire me. You know it, I know it, we all know it. Adam wouldn't have it, and neither would my dad." Eric turned to go, saying over his shoulder, "I'd recommend you not try to mess with me, especially since you're the one who's looking at charges for theft."

As Jaime watched Eric walk back inside, he closed his eyes. He breathed in and out, trying to stem the flow of emotion roiling through him.

It doesn't matter what I say, does it?

Jaime wasn't one to despair, but right then, it washed over him like a tidal wave. Even if the investigation led elsewhere, Jaime was still tainted by it. He'd still been looked at, considered. He'd been doubted. And not only did his sous chef use that against him, but Chris, a man he'd considered a friend, had already judged him and found him wanting. That fucking hurt.

As the afternoon waned on, Adam asked Jaime to come to his office. Jaime had no real desire to speak to his friend, but Adam was also his boss, so he followed him inside his office without protest.

Adam sighed, rubbing his eyes. He looked tired, complete with bags under his eyes. "I just wanted to tell you that an investigator is coming to the vineyard next week to talk to everyone. We've verified that money has been stolen, and now the police are essentially digging deeper to find out who is responsible."

Adam didn't say the words, but Jaime could hear them anyway.

"I'm the person they want to talk to?" Jaime asked. He gripped one of the chairs, his hand smarting under the pressure.

"They want to talk to everyone," Adam assured him. "Not just you."

"But they want to talk to me the most." When Adam said nothing, Jaime swore. "I knew it."

"Look, there are still no charges being filed against you. And I know you're innocent, because you are a good, decent man. I'm behind you, Jaime. Please believe that. I don't for one second think you'd steal from me. Besides, you'd think with all of this money you're supposedly stealing, you'd at least get a new truck."

Jaime barked out a laugh. "Clearly I'm not a great thief." He paused, stuffing his hands into his pockets. "But thanks. For standing behind me."

Adam got up and clapped Jaime on the shoulder. "Of course. That's what friends are for."

CHAPTER FIVE

"I'll get the dishes, Julia. Grace, do you want to help me?" Joy raised her eyebrows, and Grace had a feeling her brother's fiancée wasn't going to take no for an answer.

"Sure, I would love to." Grace began piling the dishes from dinner while Joy picked up glasses and serving plates. The Danvers tried to have family dinner a few times a week, although everyone's schedule didn't necessarily line up. Tonight, though, both Adam and Joy had attended, for which Grace had been infinitely thankful. Her parents could focus on someone else for a change, instead of grilling her with the same five questions.

"Thanks, you two," Julia said. "Let us know if you need any help."

"I think we got it." Joy went into the kitchen, setting the glasses in the sink with Grace following. The Danvers' house was old enough that it hadn't been built with a dishwasher, and Carl hadn't wanted to spend the money since then to install one. Thus, everything needed to be hand washed. Grace was used to it, and she found it kind of soothing: the same motions, the warm suds, washing, rinsing, until you were done.

Joy turned on the water and squirted dish soap into the sink, causing it to froth and bubble.

"I think you have enough soap," Grace couldn't help pointing out.

Joy wrinkled her nose. "Adam has the shitty soap in his place so I'm used to using twice as much." She watched the bubbles rise…and rise. "If it overflows I'm blaming you."

Grace scoffed. "They'd never believe it."

At Joy's grin, Grace couldn't help but smile back. She'd been so preoccupied as of late—her parents, Jaime, her lack of career, Jaime—that she hadn't spoken to her friend in a few weeks. Even though Joy was Adam's fiancée, she and Grace had become friends first. She was one of the few women close in age who Grace felt comfortable enough to talk to. A lot of women in Heron's Landing were already married, some with kids, and many of them didn't understand Grace's need to paint and create art.

Grace began washing dishes while Joy rinsed and placed them on the rack to dry. They settled into a rhythm, and Grace's mind was about to drift off when Joy asked, "So what's up with you? I haven't seen you in ages."

Grace shrugged. She scrubbed at a spoon extra hard, trying to get potato residue off of it. "Just working at Trudy's, trying to avoid my parents, the usual." She could feel Joy looking at her, expecting her to say more. Joy knew how she felt about Jaime, but what did it matter? She hadn't told her that she'd confessed how she felt, or about their time down at the river, or anything that had happened. For some reason, she'd wanted to keep that close to herself. It was like if she revealed what had happened, it would pop and disappear like the bubbles foaming beneath her fingers right now.

"Adam told me he saw you and Jaime together at River's Bend."

Grace looked at her in alarm, her heart pounding. "He did?"

"Yeah, you were about to fall out a window? Were you?"

Grace went back to washing. *She doesn't know what I said to him at the wedding. She doesn't know.* "Was I what?"

"About to fall out a window."

"Oh, yeah. Sort of. I tripped, Jaime kept me from toppling out the window. That was it."

Joy didn't say anything. She rinsed the glass Grace had handed her, filling and refilling it with water more times than necessary.

"You know," Joy began, "I won't make you talk about anything you don't want to talk about. But, I think I'm astute enough to know when my friend is keeping something from me."

Grace dropped a bowl, and it clattered in the sink. When she didn't move, Joy fished the bowl out of the sink, set it on the counter, and turned off the water. She placed a hand on her hip, turned toward Grace, and waited.

Grace didn't look at her. She knew she was blushing, though. Her hands were shaking, and she was acting like Joy had found out she'd murdered someone.

"Geez, do you need to sit down? I didn't mean to upset you." Joy touched her arm, and Grace jumped.

"Oh, no! I mean, I'm fine. Just kind of stressed. And tired. I haven't been sleeping." She switched on the water and began scrubbing the dishes with a vengeance.

"Did something happen? Between you and Jaime? Every time he's mentioned you jump like a rabbit caught by a fox."

Grace hummed underneath her breath. Was she just a rabbit and Jaime was a fox who was toying with her? Oh God, now she was thinking in animal metaphors? She handed Joy some silverware and then realized she'd scrubbed everything already. She stared at the running water, unsure how to answer.

Everything happened, nothing happened. What do you do when a guy tells you that it'd be a disaster if you got together?

"I'm not going to twist your arm," Joy said quietly. She shut off the water again. "But I'll say this: be careful. Jaime's a good guy, but he's…"

"Not the type of guy who'd go for someone like me?"

"Good lord, no. But you're young, and I've never seen him commit to a relationship longer than a few months."

Grace turned, narrowed her eyes. "You've been in Heron's Landing for not even six months. How would you know?"

Joy smiled. "Point taken. I meant, Adam has mentioned that *he* has never seen Jaime commit to a relationship beyond a few months."

"And my brother isn't at all biased with this?"

"Why would he be? Look, just watch out for yourself. That's all. Take my advice, or don't, because you're an adult. But I'd hate to see your heart broken."

Grace traced a line of water on the edge of the sink. "What happened to you telling me to be honest with him? Or is that no longer a good idea?"

"I guess, just don't give your heart away unless you know the risk you're taking. Does that make sense?" Joy sighed. "I'm sorry, I'm making no sense. I'm just worried about you. You'll come to me if you need help, right?"

Not with this. "Of course."

Joy gave her a quick hug, which Grace returned. But then she heard the front door open and Jaime's voice saying, "Sorry for coming by so late…," which made her jump away like that rabbit Joy had been talking about.

Joy frowned. "What's Jaime doing here?"

Grace wondered if she could sneak upstairs to her room, but she didn't have time. Jaime had walked inside and seen them in the kitchen. He gave a wave, which Grace didn't return. Why was he here? Could she never get away from this man?

She heard Jaime and Adam chatting, with Julia and Carl asking some questions. Did her parents know about the missing money? She had a feeling Adam was trying to keep things quiet as much as possible, and luckily, her parents didn't get out much these days. But it was unavoidable that they would eventually find out.

Joy touched her elbow and went into the dining room. Grace heard her greet Jaime, but she couldn't move. Instead of doing the polite thing, she opened the back door as quietly as she could and sneaked outside. Rubbing her arms at the chill, she tipped her head back and looked up at the stars, bright in the November sky. One of the advantages of living in the middle of nowhere was that you could see the constellations. Grace spotted Cassiopeia and then Andromeda, the latter of which was chained to a rock to be eaten by a sea monster before Perseus had swooped in to save her.

Grace felt a little like she was chained to a rock, except of her own making. *Will anyone save me?* she wondered. *Or can you be saved from yourself?*

She instantly felt embarrassed for such self-pity, and she huffed out a breath, which turned into a white cloud that floated out into the distance. She didn't need Perseus or a savior or even a key to unlock her chains. She just needed to figure out things—whatever that even meant.

"Aren't you cold?"

Grace turned, and upon seeing Jaime walking toward her, she experienced the oddest feeling: inevitability. It was inevitable that he'd find her, that he'd talk to her, that he'd stand next to her, his face in shadows. It was inevitable that she'd love him, even when he'd never love her back.

"I came to give Joy her bracelet. She dropped it in the kitchen and had been asking about it," Jaime said, explaining his presence without Grace asking.

She looked at him, but what could she say? So she looked back up at Andromeda, sparkling in the black blanket of the sky. She shivered.

"I knew you were cold. Do you ever have a coat?" Jaime pulled off his and placed it on her shoulders, just like he had down by the river. He didn't move his hands away from her shoulders, though. The heat of his hands seeped into her.

She looked up at him.

"Why are you here—with me?" She whispered the words, so quietly she didn't know if he'd heard them.

But by the light of the moon and the light through the kitchen window, she could see his jaw tighten. He still didn't move his hands away from her arms, though.

"I don't know," he admitted. "I just...wanted to see you."

Her heart clenched. She breathed a cloud into the cold night.

You're breaking my heart. You're breaking my heart and all I can do is let you. Her throat closed and every word she'd ever learned disappeared. It was just Jaime, and the night, and the cold, and the way he looked at her.

"They're going forward with the investigation. Adam told me this week. They're not charging me with anything, but I know it's me they want to talk to." The words seemed wrenched from him, and she couldn't help but be touched that he'd told her.

She covered his hands, still on her arms, with hers. "I'm sorry, Jaime. I wish I could help you."

He stepped away, but he didn't leave. Bereft of his warmth, she shivered, despite the heavy coat hanging from her shoulders.

"How do you do it?" Jaime shook his head, a sad smile on his handsome face. "You're the person my mother always warned me about."

"I don't understand."

"She always said that the most dangerous people were the ones who treated you like you were worthy of their respect. The people who listened to you." He looked up at the stars with her and breathed toward Cassiopeia, "The people who make you want to be a better man."

She wondered if Jaime Martínez knew he could crumble a girl's heart with words just like those.

They stared at the sky in silence. Grace swallowed, her mouth dry and her throat constricted. But then Jaime pointed, and he asked, "Do you know which constellation that is?"

She almost laughed, and she found her voice after a

moment. "That's Andromeda, the daughter of Cassiopeia. Chained to a rock but saved by Perseus from a sea monster, and then she marries him. Perseus, not the sea monster. The usual kind of Greek myth."

"Huh," he said. "It would've been kind of awesome if she'd married the sea monster, though."

"How would that be awesome? That sounds awful."

"Maybe the sea monster is misunderstood. Maybe he was just lonely."

Grace gave him a look, and he grinned. "Are you turning the sea monster into a Nice Guy who just wants women to like him?"

"Hey, sea monsters need love, too."

She reached out to push him, but he caught her hand before she could. He wouldn't let her go. They grappled, with Grace laughing and Jaime soon encircling her with his arms. But the body-lock quickly transformed into an embrace, and Grace could feel every inch of him against her body.

He didn't let her go. She felt his breath puff against her ear, brushing the strands of hair falling from her usual braid. Now his coat seemed too warm, and her cheeks heated. She couldn't look at him, but she did manage to raise her hands until they pressed against his chest, clad only in a thin t-shirt. His heart pounded beneath her palm.

Leaning toward her, she could hear his barest whisper. "Graciela," he murmured. "Graciela, Graciela."

She trembled. She gripped fistfuls of his shirt, like it were her only lifeline. He'd never called her that before. Suddenly her plain name became something new entirely, his mouth and lips and voice transforming her into a creature she had never met before.

He was only inches from her cheek. From her mouth. She closed her eyes.

He kept saying *Graciela*, murmuring other words in Spanish. She knew this was his admission that he couldn't say the words to her so she would understand. These words were for him alone.

She'd studied enough Spanish to catch a few words, but they all swirled together until she didn't hear words, just sounds. Movement, emotions. Inevitability.

When she opened her eyes, she tilted her head back, because she wanted him to kiss her. She didn't care if he broke her heart. What did it matter? It wouldn't stop the way she felt about him.

But instead of kissing her, he buried his face against her neck, against her shoulder, hiding himself. He muttered words. He gripped her close. She pressed her cheek to his heart, and the sound of it pumping blood soothed her.

She could feel the tension roiling through him, like he was fighting with himself. She didn't understand it. She didn't know why it had to be this way. But she wouldn't ask why.

I don't want to hear the answer.

His lips brushed her cheek, and then she was free. Her body seemed not her own, like she'd floated to another plane and was watching from above. She felt herself grip air where once she'd gripped his shirt. She swallowed. His eyes ensnared her, his brows furrowed. He breathed quickly. She wished she could see him better, but the moon had moved behind a burst of trees and now darkness wrapped around them worse than before.

The back door opened. They both jumped.

"There you two are," Adam said, poking his head out. "It's cold as balls out here. Jaime, aren't you freezing your ass off?"

Jaime shrugged, stepping in front of Grace, as if to shield her. "I'm warm-blooded. I'll live." He followed Adam inside.

Grace took a deep breath, glanced at the stars, and went back inside, too.

When she sat down on the couch in the living room, Joy was looking at her, like she wanted to crack her open and shake out her secrets. She looked away, staring at nothing in the corner. A sob choked her, and she wished she could lock herself in her room and cry the night away. She didn't even know what she'd be crying about anymore, but at this point tears seemed the only option.

"Well, I better go," Jaime said.

Jaime was about to leave when Adam remarked, "Wait, is Grace wearing your coat? Grace, let him have his coat so he doesn't get hypothermia."

Her name seemed strange now. She longed to be called Graciela instead. She looked at her family, and she realized she hadn't said anything.

"Oh, sorry," she mumbled. She shrugged out of Jaime's coat and handed it to him without looking in his face. "Have a good night."

His fingers brushed hers. "Thanks."

Then silence. The front door closed, and everyone around Grace seemed determined to say nothing and draw out the silence until it was painful.

"I'm going to bed," she announced to no one in particular. She stood up and raced upstairs, shutting her bedroom door and closing her eyes, trying to calm her pounding heart.

She didn't know what to think, or to feel, or how to act

anymore. She was tied up in knots. It made her think of that line in *Jane Eyre,* when Rochester was trying to get Jane to confess her feelings, about how they were connected by a string hooked onto their ribs. *And if you were to leave I'm afraid that cord of communion would snap. And I have a notion that I'd take to bleeding inwardly. As for you, you'd forget me.*

She collapsed onto her bed. The tears wouldn't come. She was too tired, too heart sore. Too full of emotions she could barely comprehend. She did, however, hear her door open and someone sit on the bed next to her. She felt a hand on her back, and someone saying her name. She smelled a light, rose perfume, and she knew it was Joy.

Joy didn't try to tell her it'd be all right, or that she understood, or that she should confess it all. Instead, she just sat with her, letting her know she wasn't alone. And then when her eyelids became heavy and she fell into a restless sleep, Joy quietly left.

CHAPTER SIX

Adam gathered the team that morning for a staff meeting. Jaime sat in the back, while the rest of his coworkers stared straight ahead at their boss, ignoring him as best they could. Some, like Kerry, would glance at him periodically, as if they could impart some kind encouragement from a look. Others, like Chris, acted like he wasn't even in the room.

Jaime rather wished they'd all leave him alone. Tired and irritable, he gripped his coffee mug and sipped the hot brew, wondering if he could call in sick because he hated every person at this table.

Not everyone, though. He didn't hate Adam. Adam was doing his best to do right by him and keep the entire town from knowing about the missing money and how the trail led to Jaime. Jaime still didn't understand how that was the case, and when he'd asked for details, Adam had grimaced and said that they were told by their lawyer and the investigator that that should remain confidential.

Jaime swallowed, watching Adam talk. Of course it was a

secret. They'd accused a man of theft and would throw away the key, all before showing any evidence that said man was, in fact, a thief.

"The lead investigator, Thomas Jennings, will be here today to talk to the staff. No one has to speak with him," Adam was saying, looking at everyone at the table. "No one has been charged. I would recommend that if you do decide to speak with Sheriff Jennings, that you consider your words and how they will reflect not only on yourself, but on River's Bend as a whole. I can't forbid you from saying what you wish, of course."

Jaime knew that the local police in Heron's Landing had brought in Sheriff Jennings early on in the investigation, mostly because Heron's Landing only had two local cops that had no real experience in these kinds of matters. Few crimes beyond car break-ins and public intoxication ever occurred in this tiny town. The last murder had occurred over thirty years ago, and few of the residents locked their doors at night.

"How long is this going to take?" Leah asked. Leah hosted the wine-tasting classes and was a bit of a curmudgeonly older lady. She lived alone with her calico cats, Patsy and Mrs. Witherspoon, and preferred feline companionship to most human friends. That being said, she enjoyed giving the wine-tasting classes and explaining wine to anyone who had an ear to listen.

"It shouldn't take more than a half hour," Adam replied, "if you decide to talk to Sheriff Jennings. Again, let me empha-size that this is completely voluntary."

Chris crossed his arms, harrumphing a little. "Why are they asking us questions when it's pretty clear who's respon-sible for all of this?"

Jaime set his coffee down. No one turned to look at him, but it still felt like everyone was staring at him. His temples pounded, a headache threatening.

"As I said before, no one has been charged." Adam's voice was firm, even slightly angry. He gave Chris a hard look. "I know this might be difficult to remember, but everyone is innocent until proven guilty."

Chris didn't reply, but Jaime knew the man wanted to give Adam a biting reply.

He appreciated Adam coming to his defense, but at the same time, he hated that his best recourse was saying as little as possible. He'd have to act like he'd done nothing wrong by being blasé and going about his business, when really he wanted to confront every person who thought he was guilty and maybe shove their face into some manure. Was it petty? Yes. But the satisfaction of getting to do something like that would be worth it.

Adam dismissed them, and the team trailed out of the room. Jaime returned to the kitchen, but it was difficult to concentrate. His head hurt, although the one consolation was that Eric had called in sick today. At least he didn't have to put up with his sous chef's behavior while trying to keep his cool around Sheriff Jennings.

While deveining shrimp, Jaime heard a booming voice outside, one he didn't recognize. He glanced at the clock: one o'clock. That must be the sheriff. He immediately tensed, ripping apart more than one shrimp as a result and having to toss them out.

He waited. And waited. He heard Adam and then Chris talk to the sheriff. He told one of his interns to finish deveining the shrimp while he worked on a sauce to go with the shellfish. His head still pounded, and he wished he'd taken some Advil before having to meet with the sheriff.

By two o'clock, the reckoning came. Jaime knew he was under no obligation to talk. But he was also aware that not talking could be seen as an admission of guilt. It wasn't fair and it wasn't right, but how was anything about this fair or right? He gritted his teeth, scrubbing his hands clean just as Sheriff Jennings entered the kitchen.

The sheriff could be described as a large man, and a very red one at that. His cheeks were red and chapped, his hands red, and when he smiled, you saw more red gums than teeth. His nose took up most of his face, and a spotty beard covered his cheeks and jaw. Jaime couldn't determine his age: at one moment he looked about his own age, and then in another, he could be someone's grandfather.

"Hello everyone," Sheriff Jennings said in a voice louder than necessary in the small kitchen. "Your boss already told you why I'm here today. If anyone would like to talk to me or has any useful information, let me know. As it is, I'm simply collecting information right now. Don't mind me, eh?"

Jaime dried his hands. He was shaking, he realized. When the sheriff caught his gaze, the older man gave no hint that Jaime was the one he really wanted to talk to. But his smile turned into what could only be considered a smirk, like he'd spotted his prey and was just lying in wait for it to fall into his trap.

Refusing to lie in wait, Jaime went up to Sheriff Jennings, extending his hand. "Jaime Martínez. I'm the executive chef here."

The sheriff looked him over before offering his hand. He pumped Jaime's, gripping it so hard he was sure he could feel his knuckles cracking. "Nice to meet you," the sheriff said, a slight drawl to his words. "What are you making today?"

"Shrimp risotto. Have you eaten here at River's Bend before, Sheriff?"

"Can't say that I've had the pleasure. But I'm sure whatever you serve will impress me."

Jaime smiled tightly. "Of course."

Sheriff Jennings then offered to speak with Jaime alone in Adam's office. The rest of the kitchen staff seemed to freeze, watching the proceedings like scared rabbits. Jaime accepted, following the sheriff out. It rather felt like he was being led to the gallows.

Keep your cool. Don't say anything stupid. You haven't done anything wrong.

Part of Jaime felt like he was guilty, though. Part of him felt like he needed to confess his sins, even though none of those sins had anything to do with stealing money from his place of employment.

The only sin you need to confess lately is thinking about your boss's sister way too often.

His heart twisted. He thought of Grace's expression as they'd stood together outside under the stars. The scent of her hair, the softness of her skin. How he'd been weak and called her Graciela, and how she hadn't pushed him away like she should've. She should've told him to go to hell. But she'd clung to him and leaving her that evening had taken all of his strength and then some.

Sheriff Jennings sat down in Adam's chair, forcing Jaime to take the chair across from him like some kind of subordinate. He also noticed that the sheriff had shut the door. He refused to be intimidated, though: he gazed straight at him, waiting expectantly, and praying that the sheriff couldn't hear his pounding heart.

Sheriff Jennings glanced at a folder filled with a jumble of documents, then pulled out a notebook from his pocket. "You don't mind if I take notes, do you?" He scribbled something down before asking, "So, where are you from, Jaime?"

"I'm from St. Louis, actually."

"Yes, but where from originally?"

Jaime dug his thumbnail into his palm. "From St. Louis, like I said."

The sheriff made a note, frowning. "Are your parents from St. Louis?"

"They've lived there for over thirty years, but they immigrated from El Salvador in the early '80s."

Sheriff Jennings nodded. He then scrawled his notes, flipping pages and pages, like Jaime had imparted years' worth of information in these brief statements. He continued to ask questions about Jaime's heritage, his parents, their immigration status, and never once did he ask about the missing money.

And the worst part was that Jaime couldn't fight against this assumption without making the situation worse for himself.

The only question semi-relating to the investigation the sheriff asked was, "Have you ever had money troubles?"

Who hasn't? he thought. It'd only been after a few years at River's Bend that Jaime had felt like he was in a position to feel comfortable with his income. Before that, it'd been all about scraping and saving and living paycheck to paycheck, if he wasn't in school or interning somewhere. His parents had lived similarly, despite his father's work as a professor. There never seemed to be enough money, no matter how many hours worked.

"Well, I can say that since I started here, I've been doing fairly well in terms of money," Jaime replied, couching his words. "If you're asking if it's a concern right now? No, it's not."

The sheriff eyed him, as if skeptical of his answer. Then he scribbled something, his cheeks somehow redder than before.

He asked Jaime a few more questions before saying he could go back to work. As he opened the door for Jaime, though, he just kept nodding, his eyes slightly narrowed, as if he'd figured out the puzzle and was just waiting to impart the answer to someone.

An hour or so later, Jaime heard Adam saying goodbye to Sheriff Jennings. It was only then that he let out a sigh of relief. Logically, he knew that he couldn't be arrested unless charges were filed, but some small part of him had worried that that wouldn't have mattered to the sheriff. He'd put him in handcuffs and haul him away to the jail in nearby Columbia, because Heron's Landing didn't have a jail.

"Hey Jaime, can I talk to you a minute?" Adam poked his head into the kitchen. His expression wasn't grim, per se, but it was serious.

Jaime nodded and finished up his work, washing his hands and wiping them off on his apron.

Is this just going to be the day where I get my ass grilled for hours? He had no idea what Adam needed to talk about now, unless the sheriff had told him that they were moving forward in some way.

Exhaustion swamped his limbs. He didn't even want to cook for himself when he got home. He wanted to order a pizza, drink a beer, and then sleep until everything blew over.

"Can you close the door?" Adam asked. He was standing at his desk, shuffling some papers around.

"That doesn't sound good." Jaime tried to sound like he was joking, but really he sounded strained and tired. Déjà vu hit him, and he wondered if the sheriff were hiding underneath Adam's desk, ready to pop out the moment he caught Jaime confessing to his crimes.

Adam looked up. "Sorry. I know you've had a lot going on. This actually isn't about the money or anything, if that helps."

Sitting down, Jaime was even more confused. "Now why do I feel like I'm getting an impromptu performance evaluation?"

Adam laughed. "Nothing like that. You're my best employee and quite frankly I wish I could clone you."

"So that means you're paying me more money?"

"Now you're just being ridiculous." Adam sat down, his hands folded. His initial amused demeanor faded quickly, and now he looked as serious as ever. "This actually has nothing to do with work. This is a friend-to-friend conversation. Or man-to-man."

"Okay. Shoot."

Adam looked like he wanted to be anywhere else but in his office, having this conversation. Jaime's stomach twisted when he realized what his friend was probably trying to figure out how to say.

Does he know about Grace and me? Does he know how much I want her?

He dug his thumbnail into his palm like he'd been doing earlier, hardly feeling the pain now. His mind whirled and his head pounded and God Almighty if his heart was about to burst from his chest.

Realizing he was fidgeting, he forced himself to still. He didn't even know what Adam wanted to talk to him about, anyway.

Adam cleared his throat, he pulled at his shirt collar, and then he looked up at the ceiling.

"Dude, you're killing me. What is it?" Jaime practically growled.

"This is the last thing I want to talk about, but I have to ask: is there something between you and Grace?" Adam finally returned his gaze to him, his expression hopeful, embarrassed, and deeply uncomfortable.

"What makes you think there's something between us?"

"There have been…indications that things might not be as they were." Adam sighed, rubbing his forehead. "Now I'm talking in circles. Look, I'd rather shoot myself in the arm than have this conversation. The thought of my little sister dating any man is something I can't wrap my head around, but at the same time, I can't stand by and see her get hurt." His jaw clenched as he asked again, "Is there something between you two?"

Jaime dug his thumbnail so deeply into his palm that he was surprised he didn't draw blood. He was torn between being honest with his friend and protecting Grace from her brother's censure. They hadn't done anything wrong. He knew that. But that didn't make the situation less uncomfortable, less potentially painful.

"I think I should explain that I saw you two, when you came by the house the other day," Adam said quietly. "I only saw a split second, but you two were embracing."

Will the joys of this day ever end? Jaime thought. "Grace and I..." he began, not sure where to start. "We've gotten closer." At Adam's look, he added, "As friends. We're friends. I was feeling down, she was being kind to me. That's it. You don't have to worry about anything."

Liar liar liar liar liar liar.

Adam let out a breath, as if he'd been holding it. "I know Grace has held a torch for you for a while now, so any attention from you could make her think there was something going on. You know what I mean?"

Jaime, though, couldn't respond. *Grace has held a torch for me?* Of course, now that he thought about it, it made sense, given how she'd always acted around him. Perhaps a part of him had known, but he'd dismissed it as a schoolgirl crush.

"I'm not going to take advantage of your sister," Jaime ground out, his heart still pounding at Adam's revelation. "If that's what you're asking."

I'm not going to dream about her, or think about her. Because she isn't mine to have.

"Okay, yes, that's what I was asking." Adam cleared his throat again. "Just, be careful, Jaime. You could break her heart without even realizing it."

Jaime almost laughed. Adam had no idea—no idea. He had no idea that even if he held Grace's heart, she was the one who could destroy him with the smallest of smiles.

"Now that this awkward conversation is over, how about a drink? Oh, and I meant to ask you: do you want to come over for Thanksgiving? You know you're always welcome." Adam got up without Jaime responding, opening the door. "I think we should open a bottle of that red we just got in."

"Sure, sounds good." Jaime followed him, but he hardly

heard anything else that was said. He knew that Adam was looking out for Grace. He knew that. At the same time, she was a grown woman who was capable of her own decisions. Did she really need her older brother intervening on her behalf? He couldn't imagine she'd ask Adam to come talk to him on her behalf.

Adam poured him a glass of the red. "So how about it? Join us for Thanksgiving?"

Jaime took a sip, knowing the answer he should give. But because he seemed incapable of making good decisions lately, he replied, "Yeah, I'll come."

CHAPTER SEVEN

Grace peeled the potatoes with such force that more than one poor spud was a mere nub of its former self. Quickly tossing the offending potatoes in the trash so her mother wouldn't see, she forced herself to peel only the brown peels.

I'm not freaking out. I'm not freaking out. I'm. Not. Freaking. Out.

"Grace, do you know where the potholder is?" her mother Julia asked.

Grace jumped, the peeler clattering into the sink.

"Goodness, you're so on edge today!" Julia plucked the potholder from around her daughter, giving Grace a concerned look. "Are you okay?"

"I'm fine. Just have a lot on my mind." Grace turned and began peeling, slowly and without destroying the potato in hand.

Julia didn't say anything, but Grace could feel her mother's gaze on the back of her neck.

"Well, let me know if you need any help."

Grace had been like this since Adam had so helpfully told her that they'd be having a guest for Thanksgiving: none other than Jaime himself. Of course he was coming for Thanksgiving, Grace thought, her face turning into one of irritation as she tossed the peeled potato in the nearby bowl. *I can't get away from the man!*

Jaime had attended the Danvers' Thanksgiving before, usually when he was too busy to get home to St. Louis or, in the beginning, couldn't afford the trip back. From what Grace understood, the Martínez family enjoyed Thanksgiving but didn't consider it a vital holiday, so they didn't press Jaime to make it back, that was saved for Christmas.

Grace told herself she could sit far away from Jaime and not even look at him. She didn't have to say anything. She could serve food and replenish plates and do the dishes and she could sink into her chair and act like *nothing was wrong* and it would work splendidly.

Looking at the third potato nub in her hand, she had a feeling she was in deep, deep denial.

"How's the cooking going, ladies?" Carl kissed Julia on the cheek before coming around Grace's shoulder. "I know I'm no cook, but I'm thinking we'll need more potatoes than that for mashed potatoes."

Grace forced a smile. "This peeler is just too peel-y," she explained lamely. "I keep peeling more potato than peel."

"Well, let your mother take over so you don't ruin all of the potatoes. You know that's my favorite part of Thanksgiving."

Grace nodded, swallowing hard. Normally she didn't mind that her father didn't help with the cooking and expected she and her mother to do it. Normally she just brushed off her father's criticisms. But today she found herself thinking, *If you're so concerned, why not actually help for once?*

Carl Danvers was an odd amalgam of old, conservative values with the occasional ability to adopt change when he thought it necessary. He was the one who hired Jaime, the one who first had the idea to do events at River's Bend, and who wanted his daughter to make something of herself instead of simply marrying and settling down. But those conservative values reared their heads often, and in this case, he had the expectation that the women cooked and the men waited to eat the food those women cooked.

Grace watched as her father stuck his finger in the gravy Julia was cooking, and then watched as her mother slapped his hand away playfully.

The kitchen felt small and pressing, the sudden sensation overwhelming. Grace had never minded living at home so much as she had within the last few weeks, when the ground had been shifting with every step. It wasn't so much a tidal wave of feeling but one that crept up on her, encircling her throat until she could barely breathe.

The thought of having Thanksgiving with her family seemed unbearable now.

"Grace, did you apply to any of the job listings I sent you?" Carl asked, plucking a roll that had just come out of the oven and biting into it. "You can't keep working at Trudy's forever."

Grace turned, staring at the sink full of brown ribbons of peels. She hadn't opened her father's email because she didn't want to work in an office, making coffee and copies and answering phones until her brain melted through her ears.

"No, I haven't had time," she answered, trying to sound like she was going to look at the email soon. "And I don't mind working at Trudy's."

"Of course you don't," he said behind her. "You don't have to pay rent or the electric bill and so you can make minimum wage for as long as you want."

"Carl," Julia warned.

Grace picked up a potato and began peeling it with quick movements. "You know I'd contribute if I could. I pay for my own groceries."

Carl sighed, like Grace were the greatest disappointment in the history of the Danvers family. "And yet who was the one who wouldn't listen and decided to get a degree in art? Didn't I warn you this was where you'd end up if you stuck to that plan?"

"Carl!" her mother remonstrated. "It's Thanksgiving. Can we do this later?"

"I'm only saying what the girl needs to hear. She made a decision that wasn't a good one, and now she's going to have to fix it. She can't live in our house forever."

Grace peeled and peeled and peeled. She tossed the naked potato in the bowl and picked up another. She wondered why the sink seemed like it was wavering and then she realized she had tears in her eyes. She couldn't wipe her eyes. She blinked away the tears as best she could so her parents couldn't see them.

How did you tell your father you didn't know how to fix the problem you'd made? *I just want to paint,* she'd told him when she'd decided to pursue her degree. *I'll figure out the rest later.*

Grace didn't know how she could say that she didn't know what she wanted to do. She didn't know how she could tell her father that she felt lost lately and like she was walking through a dark forest without any means to find a path.

"Ignoring me isn't going to make this go away, young lady," Carl said. "You need to get yourself a real job and stop frittering away your time, painting things nobody's gonna buy or see."

"That's enough," Julia hissed. "Leave Grace alone. It's Thanksgiving."

Carl muttered something and walked out. Thankfully, the front door opened and he was distracted by the arrival of Adam and Joy. Grace could hear Joy saying that she'd brought her famous pecan pie, and Adam ribbing that she'd burned three crusts this morning before finally buying a store-bought one.

Grace looked at the sink, realizing she had no more potatoes. She turned and came face-to-face with her mother.

"Your father loves you, you know," Julia said quietly. "He just wants what's best for you."

Grace took the bowl of potatoes to the counter before getting a large pot to fill with water. "He needs to keep his mouth shut," she muttered.

"You shouldn't talk about your father like that. He means well." In a pleading voice, Julia asked, "Please don't let him ruin Thanksgiving. Let's try to have a good time?"

Grace watched the water fill the pot. She swallowed. "I'll try my best."

Thanksgiving dinner was served by three o'clock. Grace didn't know why they had to eat in the middle of the afternoon or why that was a tradition, but when she'd asked why, Carl had said that was how they'd always done it. Besides, they could watch football right after (which really just meant Carl could fall asleep in front of the TV).

But everything regarding her father faded away when Grace came into the dining room, carrying the bowl of mashed potatoes, and saw Jaime standing there. He was wearing a dark green sweater and jeans, his hair freshly trimmed. He seemed younger, and when he laughed, she almost forgot that she had a giant bowl of potatoes in her arms.

"Those look amazing," Jaime said as she set them down on the table. "Did you make them?"

She nodded, her chin in her chest. She couldn't look at him, but she replied, "I used the potato masher. Mom tried to use the mixer, but I stopped her just in time."

Her heart fluttered when she saw his face split into a wide smile. "So you were listening. Excellent. I'm sure there's not a lump to be found."

She blushed, then blushed harder because Jaime had said her mashed potatoes were lump-less and it was the best compliment she'd received in ages.

"I have to get the rest of the food," she mumbled as she scurried back into the kitchen.

Jaime had been right: the mashed potatoes had no lumps to be found. Grace felt inordinately proud of that fact.

"This is amazing," Joy said as she served herself slices of turkey. "Thank you for cooking, Grace and Julia."

"Yes, thank you. Otherwise I would've had to eat Joy's burnt turkey and had to act like it was good." Adam tore a roll and then slathered it in butter.

"Haha, you're hilarious, acting like you didn't burn canned biscuits just a week ago."

If Grace hadn't known better, she'd swear a flush of color was climbing her older brother's cheeks. "You distracted me," he muttered.

Joy just smiled, patting his arm.

"I'm just glad I didn't have to cook anything," Jaime said, taking the focus off of the engaged couple for a moment. "Sometimes you only want to eat and not have to work for it."

Julia fluttered her hands. "I'm glad you like it. Cooking for a chef is rather nerve wracking, I have to admit. I was so afraid that the turkey would come out too dry."

"It's perfect, Mrs. Danvers," Jaime replied as he took a bite.

Grace ate in silence, watching her family interact. She was rather glad no one was paying attention to her: she could calm her mind in peace. She could avoid looking at Jaime and try to forget the way he'd touched her underneath the stars that night. She could forget how he'd looked at her at the wedding.

She could forget everything, if she just tried, very, very, hard.

"I heard from Gavin this morning," Julia said to no one in particular. "He and Emma should be here after the New Year." Gavin, the second Danvers child, had moved away from Heron's Landing after marrying his high school sweetheart Teagan. Currently living in Boston, he and Teagan had been having marital troubles for as long as Grace could remember. Now that Teagan had elected for in-patient treatment for her bipolar disorder, Gavin had thought returning home with their seven-year-old daughter would be a good respite for everyone.

Grace had a feeling Gavin was trying to escape his demons. She'd only heard bits and pieces about their marriage and Teagan's illness, but she couldn't imagine what they'd all gone through. She'd also heard that Teagan had decided that divorce would be the best option, although Grace had no idea if anything official had been filed.

Her heart hurt for her older, quieter brother. She hadn't seen him in years, and they rarely talked. But she remembered Gavin being the one to listen to her when she was a little girl, protecting her when she found monsters under her bed. While Adam had been the son who would take on River's Bend and continue the Danvers name, Gavin had been the odd son, preferring books to business and uninterested in doing anything that would please his father.

Carl made a face as he cut into his turkey. "That wife of his still in the loony bin, then?"

"She's in *treatment*," Julia said. "Yes, she's getting help. I hope she finds a way to be well soon. I know it's been difficult for all of them."

Carl just harrumphed. He'd been against Gavin's marriage from the start, and especially since Teagan's bipolar disorder had worsened.

Grace stared at her plate. The thought made her stomach twist, but sometimes she hated her father.

When she glanced up, she saw Jaime's gaze on her. It was understanding, sympathetic. It broke her heart.

She looked away.

As the food was eaten, wine flowed around the table as well. Grace watched as her father poured himself his fourth glass, and she winced. Carl rarely got intoxicated, but the few times it happened, it never ended well.

"When are you two getting married?" He pointed at Adam and Joy, a gray eyebrow raised. "Don't tell me you're waiting five years like some of these couples. What's the point of gettin' engaged if you're never gonna make it official?"

"Probably within the next year," Joy replied, "but we're more focused on the vineyard right now than we are on wedding plans."

"That's code for 'Joy wants my undivided attention when we're doing wedding planning,'" Adam rejoined.

"I already told you we aren't getting married down at the courthouse just so you can wear your grungy jeans and Converse."

"I wouldn't wear my Converse!" Adam took a sip of wine. "I'd wear my Birkenstocks."

Joy pushed at his shoulder, and he grinned.

"Besides," she added with a smug smile, "I'm still trying to convince this cheapskate that I'm not getting a dress for less than one-hundred dollars no matter how much he moans and groans."

Grace couldn't help but smile. She couldn't imagine Joy getting a gown that cost less than three grand, if not more. Grace didn't see what the fuss was about, but then again, she wasn't the one getting married.

"Who spends five thousands dollars on a *dress you wear once?*" Adam asked, his voice scandalized.

Joy just looked at him. "Do you really want me to answer that?"

"Well, be sure to get it done soon, you two. Time's a'wasting. Besides, we want grandkids here before we end up six feet under." Carl nodded, not even looking at Adam and Joy anymore. His gaze had turned to Grace, and she automatically slumped down into her chair.

"This one over here," Carl began, pointing at Grace, "is the one I'm worried about. Sitting at home, doing nothing, just painting away her life. Never thought a daughter of mine would futz around like that."

Grace tried to sink lower, but then she'd end up under the table. All eyes were on her—mostly sympathetic—but it didn't make any difference. She wanted to die. Crawl under a rock and die.

"When are you gonna get your life in order, young lady? I keep askin' her, but she just says she doesn't know." Carl scoffed. "If I could, I'd marry her off just to give her something to do."

Tears pooled in Grace's eyes just as Julia took Carl's wine glass away, whispering that he'd had enough. She couldn't look at anyone. She couldn't look at her brother or at Joy and she definitely couldn't look at Jaime. But when the tears overflowed and fell down her face, she got up, saying, "Excuse me," before hurrying outside into the cool afternoon sun.

She didn't know where she was going to go. Where could she go? She just wanted to get away from all of those gazes on her. Her father's words hurt—they did—but somehow the pity from everyone else felt worse. *Poor Grace, she's in a tough spot, isn't she?*

She wiped at her cheeks with harsh movements. Her voice caught on a sob and then she was crouched in a field, crying her heart out, only the crows circling overhead for company.

A voice inside her tried to tell her she was overreacting. But it didn't matter: the tears came, hot against her skin, dripping onto the ground. She covered her face and bit her knuckles to keep from making any more noise.

She was crying so hard that she didn't hear the footsteps behind her, and she didn't realize someone was there until she was being enveloped in warm, strong arms that wore a dark green sweater.

Jaime. Jaime, why are you here?

"Graciela, don't cry. Please don't cry." She could hear him murmuring against her ear. "Your father is an ass."

Her legs collapsed from underneath her. Jaime pulled her against his shoulder as they settled onto the ground, and she cried until she was sure she didn't have any tears left. He made soothing sounds, speaking words she didn't understand against her skin. She hiccupped, then quieted.

The wind brushed gently against the grass, the only sound around them now. The sun was already starting to set, and Grace shivered a little at the cold. But being in Jaime's arms kept her warm and protected. Her heart expanded until it would surely burst, filled with so many emotions: sadness, desire, longing, confusion.

Grace looked up, meeting Jaime's eyes. Only inches separated them. A voice whispered that she should pull away, don't make things worse, but she'd never been good about listening to those voices. She reached up a hand and smoothed back the hair from his forehead. It was as soft as she'd imagined it would be. His arms tightened around her.

"Graciela." He closed his eyes as she brushed a finger across his eyebrows. "Graciela, we can't."

She moved her hand back to his sweater. She clutched the fabric, because she needed to hold onto something. "Does it matter?" she whispered.

She wondered if he heard her, if she'd spoken to the air around them. The grass brushing against their limbs, the hard soil beneath them. It smelled like fall and hibernation and the hope of renewal.

Grace did the thing she'd vowed she'd never do, not after Jaime had rejected her when she'd confessed her feelings to him. She said, her voice tremulous yet firm, "Kiss me, Jaime."

It was like a dam broke within him. He groaned, taking her mouth like he'd wanted to do it for months, years, for so long she couldn't imagine how long he'd waited. This kiss made her heart crack, little rivulets bleeding through her body, and there was nothing she could do to make it stop.

He pulled her onto his lap, kissing her. He ran his fingers through her hair, down around her waist, twisting strands around his hand. His other hand cupped her cheek. Grace had never been kissed like this in her life, and all she could do was surrender to it.

He stroked her jaw, whispering something, and then his tongue darted inside her mouth and she could only gasp and hold on tighter. The only word she could think of was that he ravished her mouth: sucking on her tongue, nipping at her bottom lip, and she tried to match him but her mind whirled and her heart pounded so hard she felt a little faint.

He tasted like wine and Jaime, like desire and longing and all the things she knew she shouldn't want.

They broke to gasp for air, and then his mouth trailed down her neck. He brushed her hair away from her shoulder. His fingers had knotted in her shirt, and she felt imprisoned by his touch. She never wanted him to stop. Her body was on fire, every nerve ending sensitive and desperate. When his tongue swirled against her collarbone, she murmured his name.

A crow cawed. The sound was so near that they both jolted, and the spell broke. Grace stared at Jaime, and he stared at her. She knew she was probably red as a berry, and she could just make out a flush underneath his brown skin. He looked mussed, delicious, his mouth wet from kissing her.

He said something in Spanish and set her away from him. He stood up, turning away, his shoulders hunched.

She couldn't move, though. Her body was jelly. He'd kissed her until she'd forgotten her own name.

"We can't do this," he said to the sky.

If she weren't such an emotional maelstrom, she'd laugh. "But we just did. You can't deny that."

His shoulders hunched more. He turned and offered a hand up. She took it, although it meant that this was truly over. But after she stood, he let go of her.

He wouldn't look at her.

"I need to go. Can you make it back home?" he asked.

She nodded. Tears pressed against her eyelids, and she stuffed her hands into her pants pockets so she wouldn't reach out for him again.

"I'm sorry, Graciela."

As she watched him walk away, she wondered if she'd ever kiss Jaime Martínez without him apologizing for it right afterward.

CHAPTER EIGHT

Jaime guessed about five seconds passed before Grace ran after him.

"Jaime! Stop!" She grabbed onto his arm, effectively stopping him. "Are you always going to run away like this?"

That got his attention. He swiveled, looking at her flushed cheeks and ruffled hair and how she looked like she'd just gotten kissed *thoroughly*, and all he could say was, "What?"

She let go of his arm, crossing her own arms. "You can't just keep doing this. You can't kiss me and then run like you've murdered someone."

"I'm not running."

Grace just looked at him.

He ran a hand through his hair. The sun was setting and he was sure everyone inside was wondering where the hell the two of them were. Especially Adam. Jaime winced. Adam probably thought the worst was happening out here, but of course Jaime had to be the one to run after Grace.

"We just—we can't do this." His explanation sounded lame to his ears. He made a frustrated sound, mostly because he didn't know how to make things clear when he himself didn't know the answer, either.

"You keep saying that. 'We can't do this.' Why not? Why can't we? Is there some law I'm unaware of that specifically forbids us from being together?"

Having the words said out loud sent an electrical charge through him. He couldn't stop looking at Grace: how the breeze caught at tendrils of that dark blonde hair, or how her lips were still kiss-bruised. How he wanted to take her into his arms and kiss her until the sun went down and they forgot about everything and everyone else.

"It's not that simple," he said, his tone harsher than he intended.

Grace flinched, biting her lip. She looked down at her feet.

"I'm sorry." Jaime reached out to touch her, but then thought better of it. "I'm sorry for everything."

She growled—growled!—and stamped her foot in the dirt. "Will you stop apologizing? I wanted you to kiss me! I *asked* you to kiss me! Stop acting like you've violated me or done something neither of us wanted. Stop acting like you need to confess your sins for kissing a woman who's attracted to you!"

He'd never seen this side of Grace Danvers, and he had to admit, he didn't know how to deal with it. She'd always seemed so sweet, so helpful, so easy going. Then again, they all presented masks to the world, didn't they? People thought he was the diligent, hard-ass chef who didn't mind when the world tried to screw with him, who didn't shed a tear when things got tough.

"It's just a crush." He seemed as though he was trying to make himself believe that statement.

Now she looked up at him. "Seriously? Is that the only

thing you got from what I said? I'm not some dumb kid who doesn't understand her own mind." She sighed, loud and long, rubbing her forehead. "Men are idiots. The biggest, most useless idiots," she muttered to the sky.

"I'm sorry—no wait. Don't get mad again. I'm sorry for saying sorry." He smiled a little, stepping closer to her, his expression quickly sobering. "You're right. I shouldn't have said that. I know you really are interested in me."

"I'm not interested in you in the slightest right this second."

He laughed. He took her hands and kissed the backs of her fingers. Her irritation seemed to melt, and then she sighed again.

"You never answered my question," she said softly.

"About why we can't do this?"

"Yes."

He played with her fingers, noticing that she had freckles dotting the backs of her hands. She'd painted her fingernails a bright pink, although they were starting to chip.

"It's not about you or me. It's about—everything else. About your brother, about this investigation, about my parents," he replied.

She touched his fingers. "What about your parents?"

He didn't let go of her hands—because he didn't want to stop touching her—but he looked up as he said, "Did I mention to you that they're applying to become citizens?"

She shook her head.

"Well, they are, mostly because the university my dad works at isn't interested in continuing to pay for his work visa. I'm one of their most important character references, besides the fact that having a child who's a citizen helps their application immensely." He brushed a finger across a constellation of freckles. "But if I end up getting charged with a crime, their application would suffer, to say the least."

Grace inhaled. "You won't be, though. Charged, that is. You didn't do anything!"

"Doesn't mean the sheriff couldn't file trumped up charges if he wanted to."

She shook her head, pressing his fingers harder, like she wouldn't let him go. "I know I sound naïve to you," she said, "but I refuse to believe it won't all end with you being declared innocent. I know Adam is on your side. How can they charge you without evidence?"

He smiled a little sadly. He brushed a hand down her cheek. "I wish I could look at the world like you can, Graciela."

"Don't." She looked away. "Don't put me on some pedestal, like I'm an angel or something. I know the world isn't fair and I know shitty things happen but that doesn't mean I'm going to resign myself to let shitty things happen to people I care about. Not without a fight."

He wanted to kiss her again. He wanted to hold her close and keep her safe. But he also felt admiration bloom inside of his chest for her: he'd misjudged her. He'd thought her sweet and even docile, but she was neither. She loved people, but she had backbone, too. And his heart contracted at the realization that someone like Grace Danvers would fight for him.

"There's another reason we can't do this."

She looked at him, her forehead crinkling. "Oh yes, tell me more reasons why us being together would bring about the apocalypse."

"Your brother, for one."

Her eyebrows rose. "Adam? Spoiler alert, Jaime, but he isn't my keeper. If he doesn't like it, he can go sit in his room and be mad about it."

Jaime laughed softly. "I agree, but he's not just my friend: he's my boss. He already asked me to stay away from you, you know." He didn't know if he should have told her that, and at the angry expression now on her face, he realized he should've kept that bit of information to himself.

"That interfering asshole!" She pulled away, crossing her arms. "That arrogant, highhanded, bossy, *idiotic* brother of mine! I could wring his neck." She looked like she was about to stalk back to the house and do just that, but she just made annoyed noises in the back of her throat. "I'm going to kill him!"

Jaime took her by the wrist. "I shouldn't have told you that. But try not to kill your brother. He means well."

"Yes, he means well to tell men to stay away from me! How helpful of him."

"Does it matter?" he said to her back. "This still isn't a good idea."

Grace didn't respond. She stared off into the distance, Jaime still holding her wrist. He let her go, though, when she didn't look back at him.

When she spoke, it was so quiet he wasn't sure he heard her. But the words were unmistakable. "I'm not going to beg you to change your mind. I'm not going to beg you to kiss me or date me or do anything you don't want to do." She took in a breath. "But I'm not going to apologize, either. Because we did nothing wrong."

She finally turned to look at him, and her gaze pierced straight through, an arrow to his heart. "You can't keep giving me these mixed signals. One second you're kissing me, the next you're telling me it's all a mistake."

"Graciela…"

"Which is it? Is it what you want, or is it a mistake?"

He ran a hand through his hair. "Both? Neither? I don't know anymore."

She scoffed. "You know what, Jaime? Call me when you figure it out—if you ever figure it out. Because I'm not waiting around until you do."

Jaime was about to let her go, but some voice inside him refused to let her end things like this. Her grabbed her wrist, whirling her around toward him.

"Do you really think it's that simple?" he said in a low voice. "Do you really think I can jeopardize everything—my parents, my career, my freedom!—for this? If it were that simple, I could give you an answer!"

"Yes, it is that simple! Us being together isn't going to get you charged with that crime. Us being together isn't going to keep your parents from becoming citizens."

He wanted to shake her. He wanted to yell and shout to the sky and he wanted to kiss her until she melted against him. "It's all tied together. All of this. All of *us*. Would us being together keep my parents from becoming citizens? No, it wouldn't. But I'm already under a microscope with this investigation. Every move I make is being watched. If people saw that I was dating my boss's younger sister, the sweet, innocent Grace Danvers? It wouldn't end well."

Grace just stared at him, her eyes widening. She didn't try to pull away, though. He was afraid that he'd scared her. He was about to let her go, but she just placed her hands on his chest, feeling it pound beneath her palms.

They didn't say anything, just breathed together. The sun was lowering below the horizon, and Jaime could feel the chill increase. But out here, with Grace, none of that mattered. He didn't want it to matter for once in his life.

"I get what you're saying," she finally said. "I hear you. It breaks my heart, though." Her voice seemed choked. "I wish it could be different."

He let go of her wrists and enfolded her into a hug, placing his chin on top of her head. "Me too."

They stood like that for a while, until they heard voices not far away. The family was probably convinced the two of them had run away together. He stepped away and said in a soft voice, "I am sorry. For everything. Goodbye, Graciela." He kissed her forehead and then walked away, not wanting to return to the Danvers' house. How could he? Now that he'd kissed their daughter, and how he longed to do more than kiss her. He'd come and get his car later, say that he got too tipsy to drive home so he decided to walk.

You can't have her. You can't have her and you need to accept that.

He clenched his fists. He stomped through the dry grass, watching as the moon rose overhead. It was gibbous, silver and shining, and it lit his way home. It was a few miles, but he didn't care. He'd walk to the ends of the earth right now if he could. He'd dive to the bottom of the ocean if it gave him what he was looking for.

Grace had said he was running away. But how could he be with her when everything was against them? When his behavior could affect so many people negatively? How could he be selfish enough to jeopardize his parents like that? She didn't understand how tenuous his situation was.

He had the strongest urge to talk to his parents. He laughed at the thought. Would they understand this? His father would just nod soberly. *Don't do anything you'll regret,* he'd say in his lisping El Salvadorian Spanish.

He felt his phone vibrate in his pocket. Pulling it out, he read a text from Adam: *Where did you go?*

He considered not answering, but knowing his friend, Adam would probably send out a search party for him. Jaime typed quickly, *Drank too much and decided to walk home. I'll get my car in the morning. Thanks for inviting me.*

No response for a few moments. Then the question: *What did you and Grace talk about? When she came inside, she went straight upstairs to her room. She wouldn't even let Joy come in.*

Jaime grimaced. He really, really, really didn't want to have this conversation right now. The only thing he was glad about was that it was over text. If Adam had called him, God only knows what he'd give away in his voice.

We just talked, is all. She was upset, and she didn't want to go back inside.

Okay, well, thanks for doing that.

Jaime had a distinct feeling this wasn't the end of this particular conversation, but he was too tired to care at this point. He finally made it home and, upon entering, he collapsed on the giant couch he'd splurged on when he'd moved to Heron's Landing and closed his eyes. He didn't want to sleep, but at the same time, he didn't want to do anything, either.

He lay in the dark, hearing the house creak around him. He dozed briefly. He dreamed of Grace, and her hair, and her smile, and then it all coalesced into a painting that he couldn't understand. It swirled in dark, bold colors, and when he tried to touch it, it started bleeding: in blues and purples and reds, smearing his fingers.

He awoke with a start. His phone was vibrating again in his pocket. He pulled it out, rubbing his eyes, to see a text from none other than Grace herself.

Thank you for coming out to talk to me. I hope you had a good Thanksgiving.

It was such a perfunctory message, especially in comparison to their kiss and their heated conversation, that he couldn't help but laugh a little. Grace never failed to keep him on his toes.

You're welcome. Take care of yourself, okay?

Don't worry about me.

He set his phone on his coffee table, knowing there would never come a day when he didn't worry—or think—about Grace Danvers.

CHAPTER NINE

Two weeks after Thanksgiving, Grace hadn't seen nor spoken to Jaime. That had been a fairly difficult task, given the size of the town they lived in and Jaime's connection to her family. But Grace had wanted to honor his wish to stop whatever it was they'd been doing, although in actuality, she'd been too frustrated with him to see his face and not shake him until his teeth rattled.

She'd had an idea forming in her mind since then. If one of the main reasons they couldn't be together was because of this ridiculous investigation, then perhaps Grace could do something to prove Jaime's innocence. At first she dismissed the idea as too ludicrous. What could she do? She had an art degree, not a police badge. But as the days passed and she longed for Jaime just as much as ever, she felt like she had to do something. It was better than waiting around, hoping things would change.

On a bright, chilly day in early December, Grace awoke to a light snowfall. It was the first of the year, and it covered the world outside in a bright white blanket that hurt to look at too long. She'd never been much for snow, but she had to admit, it was pretty. But snow or no snow, she had a mission to accomplish.

She put on her snow boots and her coat and set off for River's Bend. It was Sunday, and it was early. No one would be there—specifically Adam, who had taken to staying at Joy's most nights and wouldn't be leaving her warm bed to sit in his office at the vineyard. One of the many good things that had resulted in her brother's engagement: he actually acted like a human being who didn't work every hour of every day.

Grace had snagged the key that her father always had on hand. Going to the back of the vineyard's main building—which made her heart pound, because it was close to where she'd spilled her guts to Jaime that night at the wedding—she unlocked the door, careful not to track snow everywhere.

She shivered. They kept the heat low when no one was around, and she guessed it was close to sixty degrees in here. She kept her coat on, stuffing her hands into her pockets. She'd forgotten to bring gloves. Darkness coated the inside of the front room, and she experienced a feeling like this wasn't really River's Bend at all, but some alternate reality version of it. She shook it off. If she were going to do this, she couldn't stand here and stare at the wall like an idiot.

She walked back to Adam's office, using the same master key to unlock it. She had no idea what she was even looking for, and part of her wanted to go back home and abandon this crazy scheme. But she was here for Jaime, wasn't she? She shut the door quietly behind her before sitting down at Adam's desk. Papers were scattered across it: financial reports, printed emails, bills, other kinds of correspondence that meant little to Grace as she scanned them. She had to smile at how often her brother printed emails. Didn't he know he could save them in a folder on his computer and save a few trees?

She shook her head. She looked through the papers on Adam's desk, but she knew he wouldn't leave something particularly important on top of his desk like that. She logged onto his computer, and then realized she'd need his password. Cursing, she tried all kinds of combinations, but nothing worked.

Sitting back, she drummed her fingers on the desk. Well, this wasn't good, was it? She began opening drawers, looking at pens and pencils, and then saw a yellow post-it attached to the inside of one of the drawers.

Username: ADanvers

Password: 1122Grapes

Grace laughed out loud. Her brother really needed to work on his computer security. She input the password, and it let her in without a hitch. Seeing all of Adam's things on his desktop, she sighed, beginning to open anything that seemed important. Guilt curled in her stomach, realizing that this wasn't exactly something Adam would be happy about if he found out. Then again, she was just looking, right? She was trying to help. Nobody else seemed to be interested in doing anything except placing the blame on Jaime with no evidence.

Resolved, she read through emails between Adam and the sheriff, scanning them. Her heart pounded when she saw that Sheriff Jennings had asked to return to River's Bend to speak to the staff a second time. Jaime's name wasn't mentioned, but it was implied. *One staff member in particular is of immense interest at this time.*

She began looking at financial spreadsheets. Profit, loss,

gross, sales tax—she didn't understand it all and the numbers hurt her brain, but she could see where there was a gap in money coming and going. She leaned toward the monitor, looking more closely at one column, specifically detailing purchases for the restaurant. She started searching for receipts, looking on the computer and then digging through physical folders in Adam's drawers. She found receipts from this year, and they all seemed like your usual kind of orders.

As she looked at the invoices, she noticed gradual price increases on the same items. She frowned, wondering if that meant anything at all. Would a vendor increase the price on an item each month?

But her focus was diverted when the door to Adam's office suddenly opened. She stuffed the folder of receipts into the drawer, shutting off the monitor just as Eric came into the office.

"Grace?" he said, staring at her. "What are you doing here?"

Grace was a terrible liar. So she looked away, trying to still her shaking hands, and said lightly as she got up from the desk, "I left my gloves here. I was just looking for them."

Eric just looked at her. He didn't seem the least bit convinced, but she didn't really care. She had to get out of here before he asked too many questions.

"What are you doing here?" she asked him.

"I left my paycheck in my mailbox. I wasn't sure if anyone would be here, but the backdoor was unlocked, so I came inside." He narrowed his eyes at her slightly, assessing her. "Where's your brother?"

"At home, I imagine." She stepped around Eric, but he moved so she couldn't leave the office without pushing him aside. "Did you need something?" she asked.

He didn't say anything. Grace waited, hoping that he'd let her go in peace. A few months ago, Eric had decided that he'd ask her out on a date, which she had turned down without considering how annoyed he'd get by her refusal. After that, he'd watched her anytime they ran into each other, with a gaze that seemed to say he was still bitter about her rejection.

Her heart pounded now. Would he try to do something now? She cursed herself for her stupidity for coming here alone.

"Were you looking for something?" Eric asked. "Other than your gloves?"

She swiveled her head toward him. "No, I wasn't." She knew her voice didn't sound convincing, but she didn't care at this point. She needed to get out of here. "I have a shift at Trudy's I need to get to," she added pointedly.

He stepped aside to let her pass. As she went through the doorway, he said in a casual voice, "You should be careful, Grace. You don't want to get involved in something you don't understand."

She looked back at him. He smiled, and it was a smile that sent a chill down her spine. But she wouldn't let him intimidate her.

"I need to lock Adam's office. Can you get your paycheck and meet me outside so I can lock everything up?"

He just shrugged. "Sure."

Grace stood outside, waiting for Eric. She didn't know what he was doing, but she knew he didn't have a key for anything important. She rubbed her arms. She needed to get to Trudy's here soon. She was about to go back inside and find him when the backdoor opened.

"Got it," he said.

She huffed, locking the door and setting off. "Took you long enough."

He didn't follow her, but instead said to her retreating back, "See you later, Grace. And be careful."

Arriving at Trudy's, she put on her apron and could barely tie it because she was still shaking. *Eric is such a cretin*, she thought as she grabbed an order pad and her favorite pen. *I hope he falls into a snowdrift and suffocates.*

Her shift was slow, as not too many people wanted to come out in the snow. She served Garrett Granger his afternoon cup of coffee—three sugars, no cream—and served some tourists a plate of waffles and eggs despite the late time.

Trudy, the owner, was there this afternoon, bustling about the café. She gave Grace a once-over and then just shook her head, as if Grace were too hopeless to help.

She was rather feeling similarly about herself.

Later, in the evening, Grace heard the front door bell jingle and called out, "Welcome to Trudy's." Looking up, she saw a woman she hadn't seen in quite some time enter. Kat Williamson, the granddaughter of Lillian Jacobs, who had come and gone from Heron's Landing throughout her life. Grace had heard Kat had returned recently to help care for Lillian, who wasn't doing well at the moment.

"Hi Ms. Williamson," Grace said as she seated Kat. "It's been a while, hasn't it?"

Kat shook out the snow from her tight curls, currently worn in an afro that framed a smiling face. Kat stood out amongst the locals, with her hair, medium-brown skin, and penchant for brightly patterned clothes. Currently wearing black plastic glasses, she rubbed off the melted snow from the lenses before putting them back on.

"Grace, right?" Kat asked. "You can call me Kat, by the way. Calling me Ms. Williamson makes me think you're talking to my mom."

"Sure thing. It's a habit I haven't broken yet, the whole Mr. and Mrs. thing."

Kat smiled, her dark brown eyes shining behind her glasses. "Being on the East Coast pretty much cured me of that. You call a woman Mrs. and you'll get slapped with *The Feminist Manifesto.*"

Grace laughed. "I'll make sure to remember that if I ever leave this town."

Kat ordered a piece of cake with coffee, which Grace brought out to her. Seeing that no one else needed her, she couldn't help but pepper Kat with questions. Although Kat wasn't a new person like Joy had been, she was new enough in that she'd gotten out of Missouri and had met people who didn't know what the Boot-heel meant or the difference between Kansas City and St. Louis.

"What are you doing now? I mean, job-wise?" Grace asked.

"I got a job at the elementary school, mostly as a computer teacher. I'm actually a computer programmer, but there isn't a huge need for those around here. So I'm going to teach the children how to type."

"That sounds...fun."

Kat took a bite of her cake. "It should be something, I'll say that. Although did you know a lot of schools have gotten rid of computer class? Which makes no sense, since we do everything on computers nowadays."

Talking about computers reminded Grace of her adventure in Adam's office today. Now a different kind of excitement filled her.

Trying to sound casual, she asked, "What kind of computer programming do you do? Like, could you hack into my computer and download all of my files?"

Kat sipped her coffee, her eyebrows raised. "Do you want me to hack into somebody's computer?"

Yes, Eric O'Neill's! "Oh, no, just curious."

"Mmhmm, well, I'm not much for illegal hacking, but I won't say that I *couldn't* do it. Most people's security systems are full of holes."

Grace nodded eagerly. "My brother writes out his user-name and password on post-its that he leaves right next to his computer!"

Kat eyed her, but it was a curious look. "Yeah, things like that. There's a reason why celebs keep getting their nudes leaked; they don't realize how easy it is to hack into systems like the cloud, or their personal accounts."

Grace heard the front door bell jingle. She looked up, greeting the couple coming in, and then said to Kat, "I need to take this, but let me know if you need anything else."

Kat put her chin on her hand, smiling. "Of course."

Grace didn't get a chance to talk to Kat again beyond giving her the bill, which she paid in quarters. "My grandma made me break a twenty for her and gave me all of this change," she said by way of explanation, shaking her head. "She told me I should use it to get a cup of coffee, even though a cup of coffee hasn't been fifty cents since she was a kid."

Grace pocketed her tip before placing the rest of the coins in the old-fashioned register. "Works for me. Have a good evening, Ms.—I mean Kat."

Kat waved and headed out, winding a bright red scarf around her neck.

Grace walked home later that evening, everything swirling in her mind. Eric, the receipts, Kat, and, of course, Jaime. If she figured out this mystery, could they be together? Or would he give some stupid excuse and run again? Her shoulders slumped as she sighed.

When she heard the sound of a car coming down the road, she looked over her shoulder. Her breath caught. She'd recognize that truck anywhere, and the man driving it. It rolled to a stop when it reached her, and Jaime was there, opening the passenger door. "Want a ride?" he asked.

Grace was almost tempted to say no, but it was cold and dark and she really wished she had her gloves. So she climbed in, putting her hands up to one of the vents blasting hot air. "Thanks," she said.

Jaime started driving again, and silence reigned between them. Then, without warning, he asked, "Did Eric ask you out?"

She froze. She turned to look at him, but it was too dark to see anything beyond his clenched jaw.

"How did you know he asked me out?"

"Does it matter? So it's true?"

She had the strongest urge to punch him in the side. He told her they can't be together, but if another guy asked her out, he got pissy? She wanted to bash her forehead against the truck's console. Men were idiots!

"It's none of your business, but yes, he did. It was months ago. I told him no. End of story."

Jaime just gripped the steering wheel.

Grace sighed. A headache threatened to erupt, and she rubbed her temples. "Are you jealous or something?"

He flinched, then turned toward her. "What?" he asked.

"You don't get to dump me or whatever it is you did and then get mad that some other guy showed interest in me." She leaned back in her seat, and closed her eyes. "It's dumb. And I don't have time for it."

Jaime didn't reply, but when she felt him stop the truck, her eyes flew open. He was clenching and unclenching his hands from the steering wheel.

"I know it's stupid," he said in a low voice, "but everything about you makes me feel stupid."

She frowned. "Is that supposed to be a compliment?"

"No, I'm telling you that you make my life harder and it's driving me crazy."

"Uh, I'm sorry…?"

She watched as something seemed to snap inside of him. With a curse, he pulled her across the leather bench seat of the truck before sealing his mouth against hers.

She knew she should push him away. She knew how this would end. *We can't do this.* And yet, kissing him, tasting him, feeling his arms around her? It felt like home. His tongue slicked inside her mouth, and she held onto his shoulders.

He was warm and solid and *safe*, and she had missed him.

"I told myself I'd stay away from you," he said on a groan, unwinding her scarf and kissing her bare throat. "I said we couldn't do this. But I couldn't stop thinking about you all this time. You're like some kind of disease."

She gasped in outrage before laughing. "And you give the worst compliments!"

"If it makes you feel better, it's a disease I don't want to be cured of."

"Why are you comparing me to something like herpes? If I'm herpes, you're…" She thought a moment. "Athlete's Foot."

He looked up at her. "I'm a foot fungus?"

"Yes, and one that keeps coming back."

He smiled, and her heart melted. "My darling herpes, you drive me insane."

Grace didn't know if she should laugh, moan, or cry. Maybe all three. But when he began to unbutton her coat, his fingers trailing down her torso, she decided biting her lip to keep from moaning like an idiot was her best option.

"Let me touch you," he whispered against her mouth. "Let me touch you, Graciela. I need you."

Like she was going to say no to something like that.

She smoothed her fingers through his hair as his hand drifted down her legs, inching up the skirt of her dress. She wore cotton leggings underneath, and as he danced his fingers across her hip, stroking her upper thigh, she felt like she was wearing too much clothing.

He looked up at her, his eyes dark. He kissed her just as he found the waistband of her leggings, and then he was touching bare skin.

"You're so soft and sweet. You drive me crazy."

You drive me insane, Jaime.

He kissed her harder. She gasped and moaned and wiggled against him, wanting him to touch her lower. Touch her all over. She'd never gotten this far with any guy, and she wished she'd worn something other than white cotton panties today. But Jaime didn't even notice, and when his fingers brushed low on her pubic bone, she shuddered.

He kissed her neck. "Are you as blonde down here? I bet you are. Blonde and fair and pink and silky soft." His words entranced her, made her heavy-eyed with desire. She could feel herself getting wetter, begging for his touch. Her entire body was on edge. She could only grip his shoulders and hope against hope that he'd touch her where she needed it most.

When he slicked a finger through her folds, she cried out softly. He captured the sound with his mouth. Her entire body shaking, he touched her with such gentleness that she wanted to cry. He murmured more words against her neck, about how wet she was, how much he wanted her, how beautiful she was. She moved her hips against his finger, which played with her in the lightest of strokes.

Her body tensed. She tried to find that perfect angle. "Jaime, Jaime," she whispered. She buried her face in his shoulder, suddenly too embarrassed to have him look at her.

He slowly pushed a finger inside of her, and then they both groaned. "God, you're tight."

She bit his shoulder to keep from screaming.

"Graciela, I want to see you. Look at me. I want to see you when you come."

She shook her head. He brushed a thumb over her clit, and she could feel herself getting close.

"Yes, look at me." He tilted her face up from his shoulder, and their gazes met. It was dark except for the light of the truck's dashboard, but she had a feeling he could see every-thing on her face. He licked at her bottom lip. "Come for me."

He inserted a second finger, and it was almost too much, but somehow as he lightly rubbed her clit and thrust his fingers inside of her, it was perfect. Something spiraled in her belly, and she didn't even realize she was moving in time with his thrusts until she felt her body melting.

"That's it," he murmured against her mouth. "There you go."

A moan and a scream and a hoarse cry coalesced in her

throat until her body seized and she was coming. She felt Jaime's thumb against her clit as he drew out her orgasm, and she stared into his eyes as it happened.

It was too much. It was all too much. She buried her face in his shoulder again, still riding the wave, and wondered if someone could break your heart just from touching you.

He slipped his hand from her body, but not before kissing her, hard and deep. Desperate. All of her nerve-endings were electrified, and she couldn't think straight. She couldn't think about the implications of what they'd just done.

Finally, he pulled his mouth away from hers, his forehead against hers.

"I'll take you home," he murmured.

She almost blurted out the words. *I love you.* But she bit her tongue until it bled, hoping that Jaime didn't see the tears in her eyes as he drove her home.

CHAPTER TEN

"You, Jaime Alejandro Martínez García, are the biggest piece of shit in the entire world."

Jaime looked at himself in his bathroom mirror, and sadly, his reflection didn't feel compelled to agree or disagree with this announcement. He turned on the faucet and splashed his face with cold water until it seeped into him and maybe, just maybe, would cool off the rest of him.

Not fucking likely.

He just had to stop and pick Grace up, didn't he? He just had to have her in his truck. And then he just had to stop said truck and touch her like that and get her off and hear her breathy moans as she orgasmed, and Jesus Christ, he wasn't sure if he hated himself more than he felt stupidly pleased with himself.

It had been a grand total of two hours since their...*encounter.* The encounter where Jaime had kissed Grace Danvers, touched her, and oh, put his hand down her pants— or leggings, in this instance—and made her come with his fingers.

Looking at himself in the mirror again, he had half a mind to punch his reflection and shatter it.

The worst thing? He didn't feel guilty. Not really. He felt guilty that he didn't feel guilty, which merely made him feel even more tangled up in whatever this whole thing was. Their relationship? Is this what this was? If you got a woman off, did that make you a sort-of couple?

He groaned. Leaving the bathroom, he picked up the bottle of wine sans glass he'd been nursing, but when he took a swig, the alcohol settled in his belly like a lead weight. If it weren't dark out and snowing, he'd go for a run. He considered it. Maybe he would go for a run. The worst that could happen was that he fell in a ditch and no one found him until morning, and at this point, he probably deserved something like that.

He laughed, the sound bitter in his small house. Going to his room, he put on his warmest running clothes, laced up his shoes, and was looking around for a hat when someone knocked on his door.

He stilled. He almost wondered if he'd imagined the sound. Then: another knock.

Opening the door with a "what the hell?", Jaime found himself face to face with the one woman he had had no intention of seeing anytime soon. If ever.

"Grace?"

Her hair was down past her waist, and she wore pajama bottoms with her snow boots. She hadn't buttoned her coat up, and he could see that she wore a thin tank top underneath.

He pulled her inside. "Is something wrong? What happened? Did you drive here in the snow?"

She didn't say anything for a moment. Then: "Are you going running? At midnight?"

He folded his arms over his chest. "I could ask you the same question. Why are you knocking at my door—at midnight?"

"I realized after you dropped me off, I had your glove. In my pocket." She pulled out the gray glove and handed it over.

Jaime didn't take it at first, but stared at it, like she'd tried to give him a dead squirrel. "You drove here, in the snow, to give me my glove?" He blinked. "At midnight?"

"It stopped snowing," she said with a little shrug.

He pocketed the glove and then, seeing that he couldn't very well send her out into the snow again, sighed. He took off his running shoes and his coat and went to the kitchen. "Are you hungry?"

He didn't listen for a reply. He dug through his fridge, pulling out eggs, and began making Eggs Benedict because it sounded good and he could do it in his sleep. Discovering that he had some leftover bacon, he began frying that up, and his house soon filled with the scents of breakfast food, calming his pounding heart.

Cooking allowed him to think when he needed to, or it allowed his mind to drift into another place. Tonight, he concentrated on the meal, poaching the eggs at the exact temperature to create that delectable runny yolk when you cut into the egg. As the eggs poached, he mixed up the hollandaise sauce, the English muffins crisping in the toaster.

He heard Grace come into the kitchen. "What are you making?"

"Eggs Benedict."

"At midnight?"

He laughed, working the sauce. "That seems to be the theme for tonight, doesn't it?"

"You need help with anything?"

He pointed a finger to the living room. "You sit your butt down and let me cook. This is a very delicate operation."

He heard her snort as she left him to it.

After placing the bacon on the muffin, he delicately put the poached eggs on top, then covered both with the hollandaise sauce. For some added color, he fanned out orange slices on the side and then sprinkled the Eggs Benedict with a little parsley. He came to the living room bearing the plates and set one in front of Grace before sitting down beside her with his own plate.

"I hope you like eggs," he said, "because I'm not making anything else."

She gave him a look. "Good thing I do, in fact, like eggs."

He smiled, cutting into the poached egg and sighing in satisfaction. "Excellent. Now eat before I change my mind about letting you stay."

They ate in silence, but it wasn't uncomfortable. It felt... homey. Like they'd been doing this for years, and afterward, they'd talk about their days and maybe watch some TV. Go to bed.

Jaime became overly aware of Grace sitting beside him, wearing that thin tank top and her pajamas with dancing bears on them. She seemed both infinitely young and absurdly mature; sometimes he didn't know how to look at her.

When they finished, Grace lay back on the couch, her hand over her stomach. "That was amazing. I could go to sleep right now."

Jaime took the plates to the kitchen, setting them on the

ledge, before returning to Grace. He sat down by her feet and propped them on his lap. She opened her eyes, surprised, but when he started rubbing her feet, she moaned a little.

As he massaged the balls of her feet, encased in purple socks, he asked, "Why are you here, Graciela?"

She didn't open her eyes or answer. He tickled her feet, which caused her to shriek with laughter.

"No, don't! Stop! I told you, I came to return your glove."

He stopped tickling, but he gave her a look saying that if she lied, he'd continue the tickling.

"No one comes out in the middle of the night to give someone a *glove*."

She wrinkled her nose. "Well, I do."

He made a move like he was going to tickle her again, and she pulled her feet up under her butt with a laugh.

"Fine! Fine, you win. Jerk."

He just waited.

She didn't look at him as she murmured, "I didn't—I didn't want what happened, to end. Like that." When her gaze collided with his, his entire body heated. "Because I don't think it should end. No matter what you think everyone will say."

They watched each other, assessing. Jaime wondered if this was a dream. Was he going to wake up again with her name in his mouth and his entire body aching? But this wasn't a dream. She'd come here—for him.

"Graciela…" He touched her calf.

"Don't." She sat up, wrapping her arms around her legs. "Don't give me your excuses. You can't tell me all the reasons why this is bad and wrong and stupid when you touch me like you did in your truck. You can't pretend like you're going to take the higher moral ground when everything you do contradicts what you say." Her voice was breaking, and she was breathing in pants. "I don't want to hear it."

He gently pulled her legs toward him and settled her on his lap. She widened her eyes at him.

As he tangled his fingers in her hair, he said, "Just so you know, I wasn't going to say anything like that."

Then he kissed her.

He should've known that the second Grace had decided she wanted something—wanted *him*—that he'd be powerless against her. As he touched her soft hair and kissed her and inhaled her scent, he didn't remotely care that he'd lost this battle.

He leaned her backward until she was underneath him on the couch. A flush had gathered in her cheeks and spread to her chest, and her breasts pushed against her top. Seeing her nipples peaking through the cloth, he realized with a groan that she wasn't wearing a bra.

"Is this what you want? Tell me now if it's not and I'll stop." He didn't touch her, but waited. He scanned her face.

She breathed—in and out. Then she sifted her fingers through his hair and murmured, "Yes, I want this."

Before she finished speaking, he kissed her. He inhaled her gasp and slicked his tongue inside her mouth, tasting her, claiming her. His hands roved down her body, cupping a breast, feeling the nipple beneath his palm. She shuddered.

The moment intensified. This wasn't just a kiss, this wasn't just touching, it was like they'd finally discovered each other and it was a revelation. Jaime could barely comprehend what was happening. His mind seemed to stop, and it was only Grace, beneath him, soft and silky and sweet.

He kissed her chin, kissing down her neck and across her collarbone. He marveled at a few freckles on her left shoulder before he gently pulled down the strap of her tank top. He looked at her face, to make sure she was enjoying this, and the desire in her expression punched him in the gut. God, he'd never get tired of that. He kissed her shoulder as he pulled the strap down her elbow and off of her arm.

He did the same to the other strap, and then her breasts were bare to him. They were small with pale pink nipples, and he touched each one, delicately tracing the blue veins he could see shadowing underneath. She hitched her hips against him.

"So pretty and pink," he marveled. He brushed his thumb against one nipple, and he just watched as her chest rose and fell in quick gasps. He continued to circle her areola, loving how her nipple continued to pucker, like it was begging for his touch.

Grace touched his face. She shifted her legs. "You're driving me crazy," she admitted.

He looked up. Her eyes were wide and glassy. He brushed hair from her forehead, tender and gentle. As his fingers moved across her lips, she kissed them, her eyelashes fluttering.

That spurred him on. He kissed across her chest, on her sternum, inhaling her scent. He cupped one breast in his hand, plumping it, and then he swirled his tongue around its straining peak. She made a sound that was between a cry and a squeal.

"So sensitive." He kissed her breast; he plucked at her nipple. He played and played, driving her wild. When she began undulating her hips against him, he took the nipple into his mouth, sucking it hard. She yelled, pulling on his hair, clutching at his shoulders.

She tasted like flowers and honey and he couldn't get enough. He licked at her and when he let her nipple go, he could see that it was now a dark pink, almost red, and it was his turn to groan. He was harder than he'd ever been in his life, and she hadn't even touched him.

He played with her other breast. But it wasn't enough. He remembered how she'd felt underneath his fingers, and he pulled her pajama bottoms down her legs. She wore white cotton panties that only made him harder.

Grace tipped her head back on the pillows as he traced her mound through her panties. He could feel she was already wet. It would only take a second and he could be inside her. He shuddered at the thought.

But he forced himself to slow down. She deserved that. He started trailing kisses up her pale legs, finding tiny moles and freckles, and even a scar on her knee that he couldn't help but love. When he spread her legs, he found more freckles.

"How do you have freckles even here?" He traced them, the explosion of tiny dots.

He could feel her shrug. "Your guess is as good as mine."

He laughed, drawing patterns on her thigh.

As he moved upward, he kissed her hip, finding a pale white scar about the size of a dime. "What happened here?" he asked.

She looked down. "Oh, that? Fell off my bike when I was six onto some gravel. I was alone and I walked all the way home, crying."

"Poor Graciela," he said, kissing the scar.

"Don't worry: I got back up on my bike the next day."

He shook his head. *Of course she did. Brave, headstrong Graciela.*

His fingers began stroking near her sex, and he played with her. He could smell her arousal, and it was heady. He muttered words, words in Spanish and in English, and they seemed to make her tilt her hips toward him.

But as he began to pull her panties down her legs, he could feel her still. Looking up at her face, her eyes were still wide, but they seemed almost panicked.

He lifted himself upward, lying on his side next to her. He touched her face, curling a strand of hair around his finger.

"Jaime…" she said. "I have to tell you…"

He waited. He had no idea what she felt compelled to tell him right then, but if she thought it was important, he'd wait. Even if his cock was hard as a rock and Grace was lying here, naked and delicious and so close to becoming his.

He thought of cold showers and tax season and deboning trout and anything else he hated to calm his desperate body.

Grace took a deep breath. She wasn't looking at him, but instead seemed intent on addressing his collarbone. "Before we do this, you should know something."

He stilled. Had she been hurt before? Had sex been unpleasant for her? He gritted his teeth, wondering if he could punch that guy in the mouth.

She tipped her chin into her chest. A blush flooded her face as she blurted, "I'm a virgin."

He stared at the top of her head. His heart galloped. And then he rolled away from her, sitting up, and groaned, knowing that he was definitely going to hell now.

CHAPTER ELEVEN

Grace watched as Jaime rolled off of her, like she'd just told him she had the plague. That little bit of information—*I'm a virgin*—had fallen out of her mouth, and now it sat in the middle of the room, like the greatest elephant, neither of them wanting to touch it. She grabbed her shirt and pants, pulling them on, not wanting to lie there half-naked.

She sat back down on the couch, covering her face with her hands. She'd been debating since forever about whether or not to tell him, mostly because she wanted him to know she had no idea what she was doing and didn't want him to think she was some incompetent loser. But now he thought she was, in fact, an incompetent loser who no guy had wanted to sleep with. She stifled a groan. Was it her fate to screw everything up? Now Jaime would look at her like this freak— twenty-three years old and a *virgin.*

The word felt heavy on her tongue. *Virgin virgin virgin.* She hated it. She hated that she cared. She hated that *he* cared. Uncovering her eyes, she wasn't sure if she wanted to cry or kick him in the kneecap.

Jaime was gazing at her, watching her, looking at her like he didn't know what to do with her. She really groaned out loud this time.

"You know what, this was a bad idea," she said. "I'm going home and going to dig a grave to throw myself into." She didn't even know what she was saying. She just had to get away from him, away from the way he was looking at her.

She knew, objectively, that twenty-three wasn't that old, and not that old to be a virgin. But that didn't stop the intense feeling of humiliation, stripped raw, showing Jaime her soft underbelly and then having him refuse to touch her, like some kind of leper. It was rather like being wrapped up in some weird, scaly skin and she wished she could rip it off, even if it left her bloody and sore.

Then again, she guessed she kind of did have a skin covering her, and she almost burst into hysterical laughter. *I'm laughing about my hymen. I need a drink.* She was to the front door when she felt a hand on her shoulder.

"Hey, no, don't leave. Not yet." Jaime snaked an arm around her waist, letting her lean against him. "Are you upset?"

She bit the inside of her cheek. Now he felt sorry for her. She wanted to die. Pulling away from him, she crossed her arms over her chest, like she could protect herself that way.

"I'm not upset," she said, in a voice that quivered.

He laughed, although it was more like a huff. She looked up, a flush climbing up her face.

"It's not funny." She stepped toward him, her fists clenching. "I'm also not the one acting like I told you I have herpes or something!"

He narrowed his dark eyes. "Is that how I'm acting?"

She could've gladly shoved him out the window. "You know what, I don't have time for this. You think I'm some kind of freak for being a virgin, like it even matters, like it isn't some social construct created to control women and their sexuality, like it makes a damn bit of difference about who I am as a person—"

Jaime stepped toward her, pressing a finger to her lips. He then drew her close, and although she was angry, she let him.

"I never said you were a freak," he said quietly, "and although I agree with everything you just said, by the way, can I explain why I may have reacted the way I did?"

She uncrossed her arms, beginning to pluck at his t-shirt collar. It had started to fray. "I guess," she mumbled.

"You're not a freak. I don't give two shits who you have or haven't slept with, by the way. But realizing that *I'd* be your first? It's a big responsibility." He took a deep breath. "I'd hate to fuck it up, Graciela."

She didn't want to, but she melted a bit at his words. She laid her cheek against his shoulder, feeling his heart pound. "You wouldn't screw it up," she said, knowing it was true.

"Your confidence in me is flattering."

"No, I know you wouldn't. Because you'd care enough to make sure it was good. Or at least, not terrible."

He laughed softly. "I'm not sure whether I should be flattered or insulted."

"I only told you because I wanted to explain..." She stepped away from him, mostly because she couldn't think with him so close. "That you'd know why I'm not very good at this." She began fiddling with her hair, beyond self-conscious. "I'm not very good with things I don't know much about, you know?"

Grace wondered how anyone did this, especially with someone they didn't know. Not for moral implications, but mostly because it was such a baring of one's self. Literally, figuratively. Emotionally. She twisted her hair around her finger and let it go, pulling and twisting and making a mess of it.

"I shouldn't have said anything," she said finally, looking up at him. "It just ruined everything. Now you're going to avoid me, aren't you?" When Jaime didn't respond, she had her answer. She sighed. "Don't put me up on some pedestal, Jaime. Don't. I'm a virgin, not some saint. You won't go to hell if you change that status."

She watched as a grin tugged at his mouth. Then he laughed. "Have I said how much I love your honesty?" He took her hand and led her back to the couch. "You're right, though. As always."

She rubbed her hands against her pajama pants. They were old and worn, the flannel almost scratchy now. "So, what do we do now?"

He raised his eyebrows. "What do you want to do?"

"Well, I definitely don't want to go home, that's for sure."

He snaked an arm around her waist and placed her on his lap. Now face-to-face, he said in a quiet voice, "How about this? You do what you'd like. You'll be in control of the entire thing."

A thrill raced through her, but fear also expanded within her. How could she be in control when she didn't know what she was doing?

"I'm not sure..." She touched that frayed collar again. "I don't know what I'm doing," she mumbled.

"You don't have to *do* anything," he reassured her. He touched her hair, her cheek.

But she wanted to do something. Her heart pounding, she gathered her courage and pressed her mouth to his. He didn't control the kiss—not like he had before—and realizing he'd meant what he'd said, her courage rose. She kissed him and he returned the kiss, hands encircling her waist. It was a slow, leisurely kiss, and she explored his mouth while he did in kind. He wasn't passive by any means, but he let her do what she wanted and followed.

She broke the kiss, wanting to take him in. His dark hair, his dark eyes, the stubble on his face. She touched his cheeks, feeling the roughness underneath her fingertips. She traced the indentation in his chin, the dip in his upper lip. She felt the soft hairs of his eyebrows, and how his right one arched slightly more than the left.

"You're beautiful," she breathed, meaning it completely. Her fingers traced down his throat, feeling his Adam's apple bob.

He smiled, brushing her hair from her face. "Shouldn't I be saying that to you?"

She shook her head. "This is about you, not me."

He let her touch, let her play. She kissed him on the soft skin behind his ear. She asked him about a scar on his jaw—shaving when he was eight and being an idiot, he replied—and asked him about a bump on his left ear. "I tried to pierce my ear in seventh grade," he said, rolling his eyes. "But it got infected two days later, and my mom said I deserved it for being so stupid."

Grace laughed. "I can't imagine you with an earring. You'd look like a pirate."

"Better than a boy band reject."

She kissed him over his heart, and for some reason, hearing him groan in his throat emboldened her. Conversation vanished. She kissed him as she touched him underneath his t-shirt. She traced the lines of his abdominals, the scattering of hair around his belly button, and then she pulled his shirt over his head. Heat spread through her as she gazed at him. A light amount of chest hair covered his pectorals, and she brushed a finger across a dark brown nipple. She'd never been this close to a man, touched one like this. It was a heady feeling. She watched as he took in deep breaths, his chest rising and falling. She smiled when she noticed a small mole close to his belly button.

His hands gripped her waist a little bit harder, like he was restraining himself. But Grace forgot all about that when she looked down and saw how hard he was, and for her. She felt dizzy realizing it. Curious but unsure, she looked at him, as if she could telepathically ask if she could touch him.

His eyes were so dark they seemed completely black.

"Can I?" she whispered.

His smile was dark and seductive. "Whatever you want, Graciela. I'm yours to command."

For some reason, looking was more intense than touching. She kissed him as her fingers roved below the waistband of his running pants. Her heart pounded so hard she could feel it in her ears. The kissing and touching became almost too much, and she pulled away, concentrating on below. Pulling his waistband down, she couldn't catch her breath. This was Jaime, almost bared to her. Jaime, who'd she'd dreamt about for so many years.

His scent, his warmth, the sounds of his breathing, the way

his hands roamed up under her shirt when he'd said he'd let her lead, all of it combined to make her braver than she'd thought possible. She stroked him through his boxers; he groaned and cursed underneath his breath.

She loved that. She never thought she could drive a man wild—let alone this man—and she felt drunk on that power. She slowly uncovered him, revealing his hard cock, and her heart stuttered. She had no basis for comparison, but he seemed large. She lightly touched the tip, then stroked a finger up and down, tracing a vein underneath the soft skin.

"Graciela," he groaned, "you're going to kill me."

She took him in her hand, squeezing gently. He cursed again. She kept doing that—squeezing, then pulling, feeling him get even harder. Fluid leaked from the tip, and when she touched her tongue to it, she felt him jerk.

His hand covered hers, and he squeezed it harder. "Like this," he said into her hair. "You can't hurt me."

She wasn't so sure, but with his hand around her own, she began moving her hand up and down, harder than before. He tilted his hips toward her. She breathed his name, and it was like that broke his control. He captured her mouth and kissed her hard, his tongue delving into her mouth as she stroked him, over and over again. She felt him tremble. He held her still as he kissed her like a wild man, and then on the last stroke of her hand and his hand upward, he cursed against her mouth. He shuddered, and she felt him coming, wetness coating her fingers.

Grace didn't stop kissing him. She tasted his pleasure, reveling in the fact that she'd done this to him. She'd gotten Jaime to lose control. She smiled against his lips, finally taking her hand from his cock, but she didn't stop touching him, either.

"Graciela, Graciela, you drive me insane," he muttered against her neck. He licked her throat, nipped at her collarbone. She didn't want him to stop touching her. She never wanted to leave his house, his lap, she never wanted to be without him.

But his kisses began to ease, and he eventually stopped, gazing at her.

"It's late," he said.

She picked up her phone from the coffee table and saw that it was close to three o'clock in the morning. She needed to get home before her parents realized she was gone. She was an adult, but being under their roof blurred the lines, too.

Standing up, she went to the bathroom to rinse off her hands before putting on her coat and boots. Looking out, she saw there was a decent amount of snow on her car, even though it had stopped snowing when she'd arrived.

"I'll drive you home," Jaime said.

She smiled, shaking her head. "And leave my car here? I'll be okay."

"Let me at least help you get the snow off."

After brushing off the powdery snow, Jaime stood outside her car door, as if he didn't want to say goodbye. Grace didn't know what to say. Did she say thank you? I'll see you soon? But then he leaned down, kissed her, and told her good night and to text him when she got home. She nodded.

She drove slowly, mostly because her mind wouldn't stop going over every detail of that night, but also because the roads were rather slick with snow. She finally got home twenty minutes later, making sure to turn off her headlights before parking her car so she wouldn't alert her parents. It was silly—she had a right to go where she wanted—but she didn't want a lecture, either.

After quietly entering, not turning on a light, she almost jumped out of her skin when she heard a voice in the living room say, "Grace?"

She edged into the room, seeing her father sitting on the couch. He looked like he'd been waiting for her. She unwound her scarf from her neck. "What are you doing up?" she asked, feeling stupid for feeling like she was caught red-handed.

"I'd like to ask the same of you," he said, shutting the book he'd been reading. "Where were you tonight?"

As she placed her coat in the hall closet and took off her boots, she found herself bristling at his question. "I don't see how that's any of your business. I'm going to bed," she replied, turning to go upstairs.

"It is my business when your mother and I are paying your bills and providing you with a roof over your head." He didn't get up, but his voice stopped her from going to her bedroom. "You have no leg to stand on, young lady."

Grace gritted her teeth. She entered the living room, her arms crossed. "I'm not some teenager. I'm an adult. I can go where I please."

"Yes, you can. You can do whatever you want. But that doesn't mean I'm not going to say anything about it. When are you going to get your act together? Sneaking out at all hours of the night while working at a dead-end job at a diner? Is this the kind of life you want?"

She hugged herself, feeling exhaustion swamp her limbs. Did her father have to constantly remind her how much of a failure she was? "I'm sorry I kept you up," she said in a quiet voice. "I'm going to sleep."

"You didn't answer my question: what are you doing with your life, Grace?"

She dug her fingers into her back. The ultimate question, and one she couldn't answer. All of the pleasure, the joy of the past few hours evaporated. Biting the inside of her cheek, she replied, "Good night, Dad."

She hurried upstairs, closing her door and locking it, like she could keep out her father's questions. Everything collided until she felt tears falling down her cheeks: Jaime's kisses, his touch, how much she'd wanted him. How she felt lost and useless and confused about her life in general. How she wanted to paint but couldn't even manage that anymore.

She wiped at the tears, collapsing onto her bed. She inhaled her shirt, smelling Jaime on it. It calmed her. The knot in her belly unraveled a little.

Even if she couldn't get her life in order, she thought, she could help Jaime get his back. She could find evidence that he was innocent. She could help him—she knew she could. She imagined his face when she told him this, and it allowed her to fall asleep, her heart not as heavy as it would've been otherwise.

CHAPTER TWELVE

Despite the investigation, River's Bend ran as it ever did. Now approaching Christmas, Jaime and the staff prepared their holiday menu, which generally brought in a decent amount of revenue before the close of the year. He worked with Adam on what to serve, ordered the necessary food, and showed his interns and chefs new techniques and recipes. Even Eric seemed somewhat engaged, although Jaime didn't expect that would last very long.

Showing his staff how to make the best rack of lamb one afternoon, Jaime found himself in a better mood than he had in ages. Mostly because he couldn't stop thinking about Grace or what had happened in his house just a few days prior. He knew he should feel guilty about it. He'd told himself he wouldn't get involved with her further, that it would only result in difficulties for him at work.

But his cheery mood wouldn't let him be plagued by guilt and doubts. For now, he was going to enjoy this small bit of happiness, especially since the investigation had yet to be resolved.

After letting the rack of lamb rest for a few minutes, he gathered his staff around him to show them how it should look. "You want it as rare as you can manage it," he said, cutting between each bone, showing them the dark pink centers. "Overcooked lamb is a terrible thing."

Everyone oohed looking at the lamb, juicy and smelling heavenly. Jaime placed each piece on a plate and let them eat it with the mint chutney he'd prepared along with it.

"When you're finished," he said, looking at all of them, "I want you to pair up into groups of threes to prepare your own lamb. I'd let you each cook your own, but we can't really afford it right now." He smiled wryly. "Be sure you don't mess up, otherwise Adam will have my neck for wasting food."

Watching his staff get to work, first scoring the fat on the lamb before searing it in hot olive oil, Jaime could only hope against hope that he wouldn't have to leave this place. That the investigation would lead away from him and he could move on with his life. When he'd first arrived at River's Bend five years ago, he had never expected it would burrow into his heart like it had. But it had become home, and the people here had become like family. The Danvers in particular—Adam, his parents. Grace.

Jaime swallowed. He never would have thought Grace Danvers would've taken hold of him like she had. When he'd first met her, she'd been a shy kid, fresh out of high school. She'd barely said two words to him before she'd left for college. Now everything had changed.

Realizing he needed to tell Kerry to order some supplies, he left the kitchen to stop by her desk. "I know we aren't swimming in cash at the moment," he said, "but I also can't run a kitchen without basic things like olive oil and aluminum foil."

She nodded, making a note on a Post-it. "You got it. I'll get approval from Adam and get it ordered. Although it might have to be the cheaper olive oil, sorry to say."

"Whatever you have to do."

Right then, Adam stepped out, and when he saw Jaime, he didn't greet him. His brows came together, and if Jaime weren't in a good mood, he'd think his friend wasn't happy to see him.

Adam stepped up to Kerry, telling her he was going to be in on a conference call within the next hour. Then he nodded at Jaime, saying his name in a low voice before going back to his office.

Jaime stared after him. Adam had never been the talkative type, to be sure, but he'd never given him the cold shoulder quite this blatantly. A frisson of fear crawled up his spine. Was there something new about the investigation? Did Adam think he stole from River's Bend now?

He looked to see Kerry frowning. "That was weird," she said.

"Maybe he and Joy had a fight."

She shook her head, tapping her pen against the desk. "I just saw Joy this morning, and she was happy as usual." She smiled a little sheepishly. "And I may have accidentally seen Adam kissing her before she left."

So it was just Jaime that Adam wasn't too fond of. He clenched his jaw and walked toward his boss's office, refusing to have another person at the vineyard treating him like some kind of leper.

He pushed open Adam's office door and saw his boss

reading over some document, his brow furrowed in concentration. When he saw Jaime standing in front of him, that brow furrow didn't disappear. Instead, it only deepened.

Jaime shut the door. "Okay, what is it this time? Have you discovered that I murdered an old lady or something?"

Adam blinked. He set down the paper in his hand and then rubbed his forehead. "Jaime, I have a conference call in the next few minutes—"

"It can wait. Tell me why you're giving me the cold shoulder and I'll leave you alone." His initial good mood evaporated much like steam. So much for having a good day, he thought bitterly.

When Adam didn't automatically disclaim giving him the cold shoulder, Jaime started pacing the small confines of the office. Adam watched him and then, after some moments, said irritably, "Stop doing that. You're making me antsy."

"Then spit it out!"

Jaime heard him mumble something about "I don't have time for this," before he looked up and said point blank, "I know about Grace going to your place."

Jaime froze. He'd expected a lot of things to come out of Adam's mouth, but this one hadn't been one of them. He wasn't sure why. Adam had warned him away from Grace before, and Heron's Landing was a tiny town. Nothing was ever kept secret for very long.

Jaime crossed his arms. "And you have a problem with that…?"

Adam scowled. "Didn't I ask you to leave her alone? What was she doing at your house in the middle of the night?" His scowl turned deeper. "You know what, on second thought, don't tell me. I don't want to know."

"Nothing happened." *Only sort of a lie, at any rate.*

"Jaime, you're my friend. You're a good man. But I know you. You aren't going to stick around; you're going to break Grace's heart. I can see it from a mile away."

Now it was Jaime's turn to scowl. "Since when do you know what I'm going to be doing? You're so convinced that I'm some amoral dickwad that I'd screw your sister and then leave her a week later?"

"Jesus Christ, please let's not talk about *screwing* my sister."

"No, let's. Because this is what this is about, isn't it?" Anger filled every vein, until Jaime barely recognized what he was saying or thinking. All he saw was a haze of red. "You've decided that I'm not good enough for your sister, so you're making it seem like you're protecting her. When, by the way, she's an adult who can make her own decisions. She doesn't need you to swoop in like some knight in shining armor."

Adam stared at him, his eyes wide. Then he got up, pressing his palms to his desk. "So you're saying you're not going to leave her alone?"

"Only if she asks me to. Only if she wants to end things. But I have a bit of news for you, buddy." Jaime leaned toward him. "It's none of your business. It never has been, and never will be."

"It is my business because she's my sister." Adam's voice was low, harsh, and if they weren't at work, Jaime had a feeling this could come to blows. He rather wished it would. It would probably make them both feel better.

"Yes, she's your sister, who's an adult. She doesn't need you making her decisions behind her back."

The two of them breathed hard, staring each other down, wondering who would give in first. Jaime refused to give in.

He refused to apologize because he'd done nothing wrong. Yes, he'd told him—and Grace—their relationship wasn't necessarily the wisest idea, but that didn't make it right for someone else to forbid it from happening, either.

"Go to hell," Jaime said before stalking out of Adam's office, shutting the door probably more loudly than necessary.

The rest of the day devolved from there. Two of the groups either burned or grossly overcooked their racks of lamb, rendering them inedible. The only bright spot was that Jaime had scheduled to leave early since it was a standard night and leave Eric in charge. He normally hated leaving Eric in charge of the rest of the staff, but by five o'clock, he didn't care. He couldn't stay one more second at River's Bend and have Adam breathing down his neck, just waiting for him to do something else to reprimand him for.

Driving home, Jaime was looking forward to an evening of booze and maybe watching a game or two, but when he got within eyeshot of his house, he knew that wasn't going to happen. Two police cars waited outside for him. Parking, he got out of his truck and, seeing four officers waiting at his door, he raised his hands in surrender.

This is it, he thought. *They're going to arrest me for a crime I didn't commit. I should've known this would happen.*

But instead of the officers coming toward him with handcuffs, only one came forward. It was Sheriff Jennings. He handed Jaime a document and said in an exultant voice, "We have authorization to search your residence, Mr. Martínez. Glad you arrived so soon. Wouldn't want to wait around all night for you to come home." He grinned, showing crooked teeth in his red and wrinkled face.

Jaime stared at the official document in his hand, glancing at the various signatures scrawled at the bottom. He swallowed.

"I'll let you in then," he said in a quiet voice, gripping his keys in his fist.

After that, he said nothing else. He said nothing as he wondered where he should sit as the officers scoured his house, going through every room, every cabinet, every drawer. He wondered if it would be strange if he turned on the TV while they worked. Would they hold that against him if he were later charged? Would they say he wasn't taking things seriously if he turned on a game? So he turned on nothing, staring at the wall, listening to the officers talking and going through everything he owned.

He didn't know what they expected to find. Then again, for all Jaime knew, someone had planted evidence without his knowledge. A smoking gun, a bloody knife, anything. Nothing would surprise him at this point. The only question he wanted answered was who would do this to him in the first place.

His second concern? His parents could never, ever find out that this happened.

The search was over faster than Jaime had expected. He watched as the officers carried out various items, including his laptop. Sheriff Jennings gave him a list of things confiscated and said they would talk with him shortly after they had finished looking through everything. Jaime nodded, not getting up to see them out.

He listened as they started their cars and finally drove off. They'd left the front door open, he realized. He went to shut it, using the bolt lock, and it was only then that the severity of what had happened collapsed upon him.

Going through his house, he looked at where the officers had opened drawers, dumped open boxes, sifted through his clothes. A pile of shoes lay at the foot of his bed, while socks and underwear were scattered across the comforter. They'd even looked through his bathroom: toothpaste tubes and his toothbrush and razor and aftershave all dumped into the sink, some of it leaking down the drain. He tightened the cap on a few items.

Sitting back down on the couch, he heard a vague buzzing in his ears. His house didn't seem like his house anymore. He took out his phone—thanking God they hadn't taken that, too—and texted Grace before he realized what he was even doing.

Where are you?

He waited. Then the reply: *I'm at Joy's. I couldn't stay at home right now. Why?*

He didn't really want to be around Joy right now, but where else could he go? He could get a room at the one inn in Heron's Landing, but he didn't want to alert the entire town that something was wrong. He couldn't stay at Adam's, either.

Can I come by tonight? I can't stay here at home.

His phone rang, and picking it up, he heard Grace ask, "Jaime, what happened? Are you all right?"

"I can't explain right now. Would Joy mind if I came by?"

Silence, before Grace said in a soft voice, "She's not here. She's with Adam. She said I could stay here tonight, though."

"I'll be there in a bit."

Parking in front of Mike's general store, he took the back stairs up to the apartments. He'd never been to Joy's, but everyone pretty much knew where everyone else lived in a small town like this. He realized, though, that he didn't know the apartment number. Staring down the hallway, he was about to call for Grace when a door at the end of the hall opened.

Grace came out, her face drawn, wearing yoga pants and a fuzzy sweater.

His heart clenched in his chest. He walked down the hallway and before either of them said a word, he took her into his arms. She wrapped her arms around his neck and he hugged her so hard he knew he was probably making it hard for her to breathe. But she didn't protest. She just said his name, over and over again, touching his back and his hair and his face.

He walked her backward into the apartment, kicking the door shut behind them. His hands roved down her back and grabbed her ass, his mouth trailing kisses across her cheeks, her nose, down her pale throat. He'd never experienced anything this intense, this desperate. It was like they couldn't stop touching each other. He never wanted to let her go.

"Kiss me, Jaime. Kiss me," she breathed, and he wondered why he'd been waiting to kiss her. Maybe because it meant making this *real*, realer than it had been up until this point. Maybe because once he kissed her he'd never, ever stop, and that thrilled him as much as it scared him.

"God, Graciela." He kissed her, and she tasted so sweet and so much like home that it was almost unbearable. She made little noises in the back of her throat as they kissed. He kissed her until he'd pushed her up against a wall, unzipping her jacket-sweater-thing and pulling it off of her, needing to feel her skin. She wore a t-shirt underneath, and he stroked her waist through the thin cotton.

"Are we going to do this?" he asked, because he had to know. He had to make sure she wanted this, because he knew he'd reached his limit.

Grace gazed at him, her eyes wide and shining. The moment slowed as she stroked his cheek, her fingers soft and light. She smelled like flowers and innocence. She seemed like she needed to see something in him, needed to ascertain some quality that he couldn't begin to comprehend, and he let her. He waited. He'd wait eternity for her, he realized.

"I love you," she said, a slight flush brushing across her freckled cheeks. "I've loved you for years. Did you know that?"

He had known. He hadn't want to acknowledge that he'd known, and he'd initially dismissed it as a young girl's crush. But gazing into her eyes, seeing the love shining on her face, all he could feel now was humility at someone like her loving someone like him. He didn't deserve it. It almost sent him to his knees.

He almost blurted something stupid—*thank you* or even worse, *I know,* like Han Solo—so instead, he pressed his forehead to hers, trying to catch his breath.

When the words came, he hadn't known they were even in his mind. But they rang truer than anything he'd said in a long time.

"You shatter me, Graciela."

Her eyes widened. Then she took his hands and kissed his fingers, and God Almighty, that was it. That was the end. His self-control snapped. Burying his hands in her long blonde hair, he tilted her head upward and kissed her, hard and relentlessly, and he could only cry out in relief that she returned the kiss with as much enthusiasm.

He walked her backward into the bedroom. A stray thought wandered into his mind, wondering if Joy would be at all happy that they were going to have sex on her bed, when Grace put his fears to rest, like she could read his mind.

"Joy said it was okay that I had guests," Grace said into his ear. He felt her smile then. "And then she sent me a text full of eggplant emojis and eyeballs. In case you were wondering."

At that, he tilted his head back and laughed. Then he fell onto the bed with Grace, kissing her until neither of them could catch their breaths.

CHAPTER THIRTEEN

Grace could hardly believe this was happening. Jaime, kissing her, on a bed, about to have sex with her. It was a dream. It was unbelievable. She could barely catch her breath. He wouldn't stop kissing her, his hands all over her, making her hot and desperate, like her skin had become too tight.

"Are you sure about this?" he asked again, although as he said it, he was inching her shirt up over her head.

"Is it cheesy to say I haven't been surer of anything in my life?"

He stilled, gripping the hem of her shirt, like he had to take in her words. He was breathing hard, and she wondered if he were having second thoughts. Was he freaked out by the fact that she was a virgin? Was *he* a virgin? She almost laughed. She knew he wasn't. He'd had his share of girlfriends, which, at that thought, jealousy pricked her, sharp and unexpected. Other women had touched him, kissed him, felt him moving inside of them. Saw his smile, how his dark hair fell across his forehead.

She took his hand, still gripping her t-shirt, and sat up. She pulled the shirt off over her head. She wasn't wearing a bra, and the cool air of the room made her nipples pucker.

Jaime groaned. "Jesus, Graciela." He pulled her into his lap, kissing and licking at her mouth, his fingers playing with her breasts.

She looked down. The contrast of his brown skin against her pale skin made her shudder. He flicked her nipples, strumming her like an instrument. She arched. He kissed her neck, his tongue hot and wet as it traced the line of her throat.

But it wasn't enough. She reached down to pull his shirt off, because she wanted him as bare as she was. He smiled a little and then his chest was bared to her. She pressed her breasts against him, and she moaned at the prickle of his chest hair against her aching nipples. It was like she was pure sensation, only alive right this moment to feel Jaime against her, over her, beneath her, their bodies entwining until neither knew where they began and ended.

He tipped her over onto the bed. She bounced a little, giggling. Then she moaned again as he kissed down her belly. She couldn't catch her breath. She'd never done any of this before with a man, and if she thought about it too much, she knew she'd get overwhelmed. But she told herself it was Jaime. It was Jaime, and she trusted him.

"You're so soft," he rumbled, caressing her belly. "How are you so soft?"

She laughed. "I don't know, good genetics?"

"Whatever it is, it's driving me insane. I could touch you for hours."

She gasped in a breath when he touched her sides, and he looked up at her, remembering how ticklish she was.

"Don't you dare," she warned, pressing a foot against his side.

He danced his fingers on that ticklish patch of skin, and she burst out laughing. She curled in on herself, trying to get away, but he was relentless. Knowing she had to be quick, she hitched a leg over his hip and using her weight, flipped him onto his back so she straddled him. She took hold of his hands.

"Now you're my prisoner," Grace said, cuffing his hands with her fingers. She knew he could get away if he wanted to. But he didn't.

He lay beneath her, gazing at her, and she could feel his hardness against her ass. It was an unfamiliar pressure, but one that sent sparks up her entire body. She wanted this. She wanted *him*.

Slowly, she let go of his wrists, but instead of freeing him, she placed his hands onto her breasts.

"Touch me," she said. "Please."

He growled, pulling her down for a kiss. Then he moved her upward until her breasts dangled in front of his mouth and he sucked a nipple, and she almost screamed. His tongue worked her nipple, licking and sucking and Grace didn't even realize she was moving her lower body against him, trying to find some kind of friction. He moved to her other breast, plucking at the reddened nipple.

She couldn't bear it. She felt like her body was on fire, about to explode.

"I'm ready," she gasped out as he kept kissing her breasts. "Please, Jaime."

He tipped her over again, taking control. He kissed her chin, her jaw. She felt his fingers on the waistband of her yoga pants, and then cool air as he took them off. Clad only in her panties, she couldn't even be embarrassed that she was almost naked underneath him. Any virginal modesty had disappeared under a haze of need.

He spread her legs, running his index finger along her sex. She arched her hips, needing more—more of everything. Leaning down, he kissed her there, and she could feel his hot breath through her panties.

Grace was sure she was as ready as she'd ever be. She wanted to tell him to get on with things, to stop playing, to stop making her desperate, but she forgot all of that when he hooked his fingers underneath the waistband of her panties and tugged them down her legs. Completely exposed, she instinctively tried to cross her legs. This was too much. What would he even think of her? What if he didn't like it?

Jaime sat up, kissing her knees. He caressed her legs, gentle, not pushing.

"Are you all right?" he asked.

She didn't know. She'd thought she was, but suddenly, nerves had gotten the better of her.

"I don't…it might be bad." She closed her eyes.

"Graciela, look at me."

She opened her eyes.

"It could never be bad, because it's *you*. Do you believe me?"

At the look in his eyes—tenderness, concern, desire—all she could do was nod. She did believe him. She had to. Otherwise she'd never get beyond this moment.

Spreading her legs, she couldn't help but close her eyes again. But that was all right. In fact, it was ideal, because then she could concentrate solely on feeling. She heard a shift on the bed, and then Jaime placed her feet on what she assumed were his shoulders. He didn't touch her right away. She wondered why he was waiting. Was he just looking at her? She couldn't bear the thought. She forced herself to be patient, breathing deeply.

When his fingers parted her, she couldn't help it: she gasped. He stroked her belly.

"Pretty and pink and wet," she heard him murmur. "I've wanted to taste you for ages."

She could only make a squeaking sound in the back of her throat.

He touched her, stroking her folds, making her entire body shiver. She curled her toes, like she could gain some kind of purchase from the onslaught of sensations. When he touched the tip of his tongue to her center, her eyes flew open, and the sight of his dark head between her legs caused a flush to envelop her body.

She heard him mutter things against her skin, his tongue tracing patterns, lightly licking around her clit. His fingers drew her wetness across her sex, readying her for his touch. She arched her hips. It was too much and yet not enough. She was a live wire, electric and ready to burst.

As he continued to lick her clit, he pushed a single finger inside of her. They both groaned. "God, you're tight," he said, breathing hard. "So tight and wet."

Just that one finger felt like too much. Grace was panting, pushing her feet against his shoulders, almost like she wanted to push him away. He stroked her, slowly pulling out and pushing back in, beginning a rhythm that went in time with the strokes around her clit. She didn't even realize she was bucking against him, but he had to put his arm on her belly to keep her still for his touch.

She was wild for him. He upped the ante, mouthing her clit now, and his finger stroked her faster. The pressure of his mouth and his hand coalesced until she could feel herself going higher and higher and higher. She heard someone saying his name over and over again and she was so lost she didn't even realize *she* was the one saying it.

Then she broke. She bit her hand as she came, her body shaking and trembling, and Jaime only made her orgasm last longer, licking at her. She pressed her sex against his mouth. She wanted all of it. She never wanted him to stop. But then it almost became overwhelming, and she sat up on her elbows, pushing away from his mouth. She panted, still shivering slightly.

He sat up beside her. She smiled, kissing him, and it was a thrill to taste herself on his mouth. His hands caressed her sides.

"All right?" He kissed her cheeks.

She nodded. "I think I blacked out for a bit there."

"Good." He wrapped an arm around her waist and laid her back down on the bed. He shucked off his pants and socks, returning to the bed to kiss her. She'd seen his cock before, but having it so close to her sex made her heart pound. She was going to do this. She was going to have sex for the first time.

She was going to lose her virginity to Jaime. *Finally.*

But as he was kissing her, he suddenly pulled back with a curse. At her look, he said, "Condoms."

She almost laughed. She didn't know why, but it was such an ordinary kind of thing to bring up in this moment that had felt nothing but extraordinary. She looked over her shoulder at the bedside table.

"I'm sure Joy wouldn't mind if we used some." Grace scooted over and, opening the drawer, found a number of foil packets stashed there. She refused to think about Joy and her brother using them, though. That was just too weird. She tossed them onto the bed, tearing one off and handing it to Jaime.

"For you, sir," she said in a prim voice, like she was handing him some important document.

Jaime laughed, shaking his head. "You're killing me, Graciela."

"You're killing me, stalling like this," she countered. She lay back down on the bed, her knees up. "I'll wait until you get ready, though."

He swore at her, and then he swore even more when the packet wouldn't tear open. She laughed so hard that tears sprang to her eyes.

"It's not funny." After he rolled the condom on, he crawled over her, pinning her wrists to the bed. "I'll have my revenge, you know."

"I think you talk too much, Jaime Martínez."

He let go of her wrists to part her legs, and that got her to gasp. He kissed her, his tongue entering her mouth as she felt his cock brush against her entrance. She was already trembling.

"I'll go slow," he said. "Tell me if you need me to stop."

She almost wanted to cry. She wanted to beg him to thrust inside and make her his. She wanted him more than she'd wanted anything in her life.

His cock entered her, and although she felt like she was

being stretched, there wasn't any pain. He placed her legs on his hips, giving him wider access. He pushed with one last thrust, and then he was completely inside her.

She gazed at him. He was inside her. His cock was inside her and she wasn't a virgin anymore. She wanted all of him though, she wanted him to take her so hard she couldn't remember her own name. But words failed her. So she pulled his head down and kissed him.

He groaned. He began thrusting inside her, gently at first, but then more insistently.

She had a feeling he was holding back for her. "Don't stop," she murmured against his mouth. "Don't ever stop."

"I won't." He kissed her neck, her breasts, his cock filling her over and over again. It was almost brutal, but in a way that made her feel like she'd been stripped bare and was remade into someone else. Watching him make love to her, his forehead gleaming with perspiration, she knew she'd never loved him as much as she did at that moment.

But then pleasure overtook reason. Her body began feeling that familiar ache, and she marveled that she could come a second time tonight. She gripped his forearms, she squeezed her legs against his sides, and he picked up speed. Their bodies slapped together, and when he ground against her clit with each thrust, she gasped.

He said something in Spanish. She took his face in her hands, and they gazed at each other as the pleasure spiraled higher and higher. A high-pitched moan built in the back of Grace's throat.

Jaime licked at her chin. "Come for me," he said in that voice of his. That voice she could never refuse.

She was coming. She was coming, and she shattered. She

exploded into a million pieces, her body bowing upward, and Jaime kept thrusting, milking every bit of ecstasy from her body. She was noisy and desperate and she felt him shaking against her as he found his release, too. He said her name and then he kissed her. She poured every bit of feeling into that kiss. She wanted him to know that everything about him devastated her.

He collapsed, rolling her over so they lay on their sides. Panting for breath, Grace couldn't stop touching him, and he seemed to feel the same. They kissed for a while longer, as if the thought of talking about what had just happened seemed like too much. So they kissed and touched and memorized each other's bodies until sleep claimed them.

WHEN GRACE AWOKE, it wasn't yet dawn. Disoriented, she wasn't sure where she was until she felt the solid weight of someone against her back. *Jaime.* A blush flooded her cheeks, remembering everything that had happened. Every kiss, every touch, every feeling.

I slept with Jaime. I slept with Jaime.

She was torn between giddiness and terror. Giddiness, because it had been amazing, and terror, because it had been amazing and she would always have that as a basis for comparison. Not that she was planning on sleeping with a bunch of other men any time soon. If ever.

She sighed, turning so she faced him. He was still sleeping, and she watched him for a while. His dark hair was a mess, and stubble dotted his cheeks and jaw. She touched his hair, feeling the silky strands between her fingers. When he made a noise in his sleep, she smiled.

She dozed off after that. When she woke up again, light was shining through the windows of Joy's apartment and Jaime was awake. He'd been watching her, and she felt self-conscious. She probably looked like a total mess, her hair in snarls. Glancing down and remembering she was naked, she squeaked and covered herself with the sheet. Which wouldn't budge underneath Jaime's body weight, so she had to give it a few pulls while he laughed softly.

"I think modesty is pointless now, don't you think?" He kissed her forehead, letting her wrap the sheet around her chest.

"Modesty is never pointless."

"Then I won't point out that I had my mouth on those breasts you're trying to hide only"—he looked at his phone—"four hours ago."

She blushed, burying her face in her pillow. He rubbed her back as she tried to calm the blood rushing to her cheeks.

"You know you blush all over? I've never seen anything like it," he said.

She looked up from the pillow, glaring. "Even if you notice it, as a gentleman, you shouldn't actually *mention* it."

"But I like it."

"You'd be the only one."

He inched the sheet down, exposing the angles of her shoulder blades. He kissed her between them. "You know you have a freckle on your right shoulder?"

"Mmm, I've had it forever."

He licked it. It was about the size of a pea. "I also like it."

"You're weird." But she smiled against the pillow regardless.

As he stroked her back, she laid against the pillow, not wanting to get up. Not wanting to face the day. Not wanting to go back home and see her dad ever again.

"What happened, Grace? Why were you staying here tonight?" Jaime danced a figure-eight around her left shoulder blade.

She sighed. "Let's just say my dad and I don't see eye to eye on a lot of things."

"What did he say to you?"

She didn't want to talk about this, especially when it partially had to do with him. She squirmed when he tapped his fingers against her lower back.

"Graciela…"

"Fine. He caught me coming in after I came home from your place. He basically said I need to get my life in order and stop screwing around. The next morning, I asked Joy if I could stay here. That's it."

He didn't say anything for a few moments. He propped himself on his elbow next to her. "I'm sorry I got you in trouble."

She snorted. "I'm an adult. I can come and go when I want, so don't apologize. My dad is just a hard ass who thinks his opinions are golden."

"Still, I hate to think that you are at odds with your family."

She shrugged. "I'll live." She didn't want to talk about how much her dad's words had hurt her. She hated to think he thought of her as a failure to be ashamed of.

"But what about you?" Grace touched his arm. "You said

you'd explain what was wrong when you got here, then…" She blushed again.

She could see him remembering everything that had happened. She took his hand, entwining their fingers together.

He clenched his jaw, and then said in a harsh voice, "The cops showed up yesterday with a search warrant. They basically ransacked my place, took my laptop, pretty much anything of value. I'm lucky they let me keep my phone."

Grace squeezed his hand. Her heart twisted in her chest. "Have they pressed charges?"

"No, but I imagine it's only a matter of time before they will."

"But you haven't done anything wrong!"

"I know." He smiled sadly. "But someone has it out for me, and I don't think there's anything I can do to stop them."

She started breathing harder, panic filling her. Jaime couldn't go to jail. He couldn't be arrested for a crime he didn't commit. She buried her face in his shoulder, clutching at him, as if she could keep him here and protected through force of will.

"Hey, hey, it'll be all right," he said against her hair. "We'll figure it out."

She knew he was just saying that to comfort her. She appreciated it, but at the same time, it only strengthened her resolve to figure out this mystery. But she didn't tell Jaime that. Instead, she tipped her head back, looking into his eyes, and said, "Stay with me?"

His gaze roved over her face. He pushed her hair back from her cheek. "Of course I will," he said before kissing her.

AFTER JAIME LEFT to go back to his house, Grace resolved to return to River's Bend and find those receipts she'd found. It was a Sunday; nobody would be there. Putting on her boots and coat, she drove over there late that afternoon. She tried very hard to concentrate, but it was rather difficult, given that her body didn't want her to forget what she'd done with Jaime the night before.

After he'd left, kissing her and murmuring her name, she'd gone to the bathroom and stared at herself in the mirror. It had been an odd experience. She'd wondered if she'd look different. Did losing your virginity transform you into a new person? Logically, she knew it didn't.

But standing there, wearing only a bra and panties, she found the love marks dotting her pale skin. She saw the beard burn on her breasts. Leaning forward, she looked at her face, like she could see some new layer upon it. There was nothing, of course. She was still Grace Danvers, still whoever she'd been yesterday. Yet she couldn't help but feel there was something different, something you couldn't name, precisely. Like a slight difference in movement, or like the light shone on her in a way she hadn't noticed before.

She stood there for a while. Sometimes it was like she was looking at someone else entirely, while in the next moment, she recognized herself. It was disconcerting. Shaking her head, she stripped out of her underwear and got in the shower, letting the warm water ease some of the aches of last night, centering primarily between her legs. Having sex for the first time hadn't hurt, and she hadn't expected it would, really, but now in the light of the morning, she felt it all. Maybe her body was just more attuned to itself, she thought.

Now, driving to River's Bend, she shifted on the seat and winced a little. *Yeah, okay, I'm kind of sore.* But she couldn't regret what she'd done. If she were honest, it had been one of the most beautiful moments of her life. If she thought about it too long, she'd probably start crying like a loony.

She unlocked the back door of the vineyard, glancing around to make sure no one was here. She didn't see any cars, and it was too cold and gray for anyone to want a tour. The vineyard was sometimes open on Sundays during the spring and summer months, but in December, it was generally deserted. She made sure to lock the back door after she'd entered.

Grace flipped on a light, going straight to her brother's office. She wished she'd taken the receipts the first time around, but with Eric snooping around, she hadn't wanted to make him suspicious. She began going through Adam's drawers. Finding the folder from before, she took out some of the receipts.

Going from oldest to newest, she noticed two things for a vendor supplying their produce: one, that certain food items had increased in price since January and two, that the invoices were all addressed to Jaime.

She frowned. Starting in March, items like apples and flour started increasing in price, going up incrementally each month. By the time she'd gotten to the last invoice, she saw that there'd been an increase of almost twenty-five percent overall. She knew that produce varied in price due to the season, but why would something as basic as flour and sugar be more expensive in August than it would've been in February? That made no sense.

She placed that folder on the corner of the desk. She then saw a folder of checks on Adam's desk and started going through them. She couldn't find anything amiss there, though, but something niggled in the back of her brain. Going to the copy machine, she made copies of everything before putting it all back where she'd found it. About to log onto his computer, she was sitting at his desk when she heard footsteps.

Immediately, she got up and turned off the light in Adam's office. She waited and listened, clutching her bag. The footsteps continued and seemed to go past the front desk into the kitchen. Slowly opening the door, Grace looked around. She'd locked the backdoor, so whoever was here must have their own key. Maybe it was Jaime? She kept listening, but she heard nothing more.

She walked toward the exit, making as little noise as possible. When she reached the backdoor, she saw it was unlocked. She turned the knob, and it creaked so loudly on its hinges she swore underneath her breath. But she stepped out and into the cold outside, almost running to her car.

She stopped in her tracks, though, when she saw the car parked next to hers. She'd know that red car anywhere. *Eric. Why is Eric here again?*

"Funny how we keep running into each other here."

She whirled. Eric stood in front of her, his head cocked to the side.

Grace tipped her chin up. "I just had to pick something up. What are *you* doing here?"

"Same thing as you." He stepped closer. "Although I have a

feeling you might have been looking for things that are none of your business."

Her heart pounded so hard she felt dizzy. "What is that supposed to mean?"

"Just what I said. Don't get involved where you don't belong." He looked up to the sky, then shrugged with a smile on his face. "I can't guarantee what'll happen otherwise."

She watched as Eric got into his car and drove off. She stood there, frozen, her hands shaking. She knew who'd set Jaime up. She'd suspected since the beginning, but this had made it clearer than day. Eric. It was Eric. She didn't know if she had enough proof, though.

As she drove away, she pulled out her phone and called the one person she knew who could help her get that evidence.

"Kat? Hey, can I come over? I need to talk to you about something."

fter leaving Grace and returning back to his house, Jaime showered and tried to put things away from the search warrant. Despite the cloud of doom hanging over his head due to this entire investigation, he couldn't feel completely hopeless, either. As he put away clothes in his drawer, he thought about everything that had happened last night.

Grace, kissing him. Grace, trembling in his arms. Grace, so lovely and wet and tight and amazing. He'd never slept with a virgin, except when he'd been a virgin himself, and he hadn't known what to expect. He'd been afraid that she'd have a change of heart or even cried, but he should've known better. She'd known what she'd wanted and had only faltered for one moment, before she insisted they continue what they had started.

He laughed a little at himself. If anyone had been afraid, it had been him. He'd been afraid he'd hurt her unintentionally. What did he know about women and their first times beyond that it was supposed to be painful and there was blood involved? But in the morning, there had been no bloody sheets or anything that macabre. Simply Grace, sleeping peacefully beside him, her hair fanned across the pillow, her ass pressed up against his groin, making him want her all over again. He'd wanted to stay with her all morning and take her for a second, third, thousandth time, but he'd pulled himself away.

He had to clear his head. He had to focus. He couldn't let her distract him.

But here he was, staring out the window like a moody teenager, his heart practically floating above his head. He tossed the rest of his clothes in a drawer. Was he going to start writing poetry now? Maybe he'd go to her window and sing her a song of his love?

He froze. Jaime was not adverse to love. Love was great, it was messy, it was interesting, it was what it was. But he'd never used that word in reference to Grace Danvers. Suddenly, it seemed like the walls in his room were closing in. It was like everything came into focus while simultaneously becoming entangled and knotted.

Was he in love with her? He didn't know. But he did know that whenever he thought about her, it was with a mixture of longing and dismay. He didn't understand the dismay: was it his conscience, flaying him for losing his self-control? Or was it something deeper, like he was dismayed with himself for letting himself fall for her.

He shook his head. Going into his office, he cleaned that up while refusing to think about Grace any longer. He'd drive himself crazy doing that. Besides, how could they have a relationship when her own brother had warned him away from her? He scowled, remembering Adam's warning. *Well, it's too late now...*

As he cleaned, his phone rang. Seeing that it was his dad, Jaime answered it while placing pens and other office supplies back into their places on his desk.

"Jaimito, how are you?" Fernando asked in Spanish.

They talked for a few minutes, Jaime avoiding the investigation while Fernando seemed intent on avoiding talking about their citizenship applications. This made Jaime tense, although his father sounded normal as usual.

Ten minutes into their conversation, though, Fernando seemed like he didn't know what else to say. Jaime heard a noise in the background, then his father cleared his throat.

"I wanted to talk to you about something," he finally said, his voice quiet.

Jaime sat down in his office chair. "What is it?"

"We got a call from our lawyer. We're close to finishing our application, but he was informed of something that could make that difficult."

"Now you're freaking me out."

Fernando sighed. "Jaimito, we know about the investigation. Why didn't you tell us?"

Jaime gazed out into his backyard, the grass brown and dotted with patchy snow. A breeze rustled the skeletal branches of a maple tree, a few large crows sitting in the tree. A chill ran through his veins.

"I didn't say anything because I didn't want to worry you. They haven't pressed charges or anything like that."

"It doesn't matter," his father said in an earnest voice. "You should've told us. Jaimito, we're your parents. Your mother..."

Jaime winced. He could just imagine his mother's face

when she heard her only son was being looked at for possibly stealing from his workplace. She'd never believe it, but the potential taint of such an investigation was enough to make things difficult. She knew that, his father knew it, and although he didn't want t o acknowledge it, Jaime knew it, too.

"I'm sorry, Papá. I should've told you. But I hoped it wouldn't go beyond just looking at me. I never thought it would go this far." Jaime felt his throat close up. He wished he were at home with his parents because right at that moment, he felt lonelier than he'd been in a long time.

"I understand. I know you. You are a good man and a good son. But you must be careful, too." Fernando took a breath. "As of right now, I don't think you can provide a character reference for us."

Jaime clutched his phone tightly. Since he was a citizen, he was one of the biggest reasons Immigration would grant his parents citizenship. He didn't have to provide a character reference, it was true, but it would be more difficult if he didn't.

He gritted his teeth. He wanted to yell at his father, but instead all he said was, "I didn't do it, you know."

"I know. I believe you. But do you see? It doesn't matter. There are people looking at you, and not in a good way."

"I'm sorry," he whispered.

"We'll get through this," Fernando said firmly. "You will, too. Know that your mother and I are here for you. Don't keep secrets from us, yes?"

Jaime smiled. "Considering you always find out anyway, I won't try to again."

"Good. We'll let you know if we have any updates with our

application. Oh, and call your mother soon. She's worried about you."

Jaime said goodbye before slumping in his chair. He stared out his window, not even sure how much time had passed. He watched as the sun set and a gray twilight transformed the sky. The crows had flown away hours ago.

When he heard his doorbell ring, he stiffened. Was this day only to be full of bad news? He went to his bedroom, peering out the window to make sure it wasn't more police, but he didn't see any cop cars. He opened the front door to find Grace on his doorstep. Again.

"Oh good, I was afraid you were out." She came in and hugged him.

And with that, his depressed mood lightened—at least enough that he felt like he could keep going. He hugged her back and then kissed her. She tasted like strawberries.

"I missed you," he admitted.

She smiled. "It's only been twelve hours."

"Doesn't matter. Do you want something to eat?"

"Maybe in a little bit. I have something to show you." She set her bag onto the floor, rifling through it and pulling out a stack of papers. "I found these in Adam's office."

His eyebrows shot up. "You were in your brother's office? Does he know this?"

She bit her lip, not looking at him. "What Adam doesn't know won't hurt him."

"Huh. I'll be sure to tell him that."

"Look, I know it's not the best thing, but nobody else seems willing to look beyond the surface." She fanned out the documents onto his coffee table. Jaime recognized invoices and checks, nothing that he hadn't seen before.

"Okay, Sherlock," he said, "what have you uncovered?"

She glared. "Do you want my help or not?"

"I'd prefer you don't get yourself in trouble on my account." She glared even harder. "But thank you." He kissed her. "Show me."

She explained the price discrepancies on the invoices, which Jaime didn't find all that convincing. Prices went up with vendors. He tried not to show that he wasn't remotely convinced, but Grace seemed to sense it. She then pulled the checks toward him. He looked through them, but he couldn't see anything amiss.

"The checks seem fine, right?" she said, her eyes wide. "But when I talked to Kat—"

"Kat Williamson? Doesn't she teach at the elementary school?"

"She does. She's also brilliant with computers."

When Grace didn't explain what that meant, Jaime looked at her. As a flush climbed her cheeks, he said, "Graciela, what did you do?"

"Nothing! Well, I didn't do anything. I just asked Kat for a favor."

"What was that favor?"

She chewed on her lip. "Just to look at some things on Adam's computer..."

"Grace!"

She tugged on his arm. "It's all for a good cause! Kat agrees with me. She knows something is wrong here. And we found a spreadsheet for all the checks that had been issued and we discovered a number of ones are missing here!"

"They could just be in another folder."

"Maybe, but I think someone could be stealing them and depositing them into their own account."

Jaime set the copies back onto the table. "And who is doing this? Do you have someone in mind, or are you just coming up with this from thin air?"

"I think I know who it is." She wouldn't look at him, though.

He tipped her chin up, making her look him in the eye. "Tell me."

"Both times I went to the vineyard, I ran into Eric." Jaime groaned, about to stand up. "No, listen to me. The first time he seemed interested in what I was doing there—"

"I think anyone would've wondered what you were doing."

"Yes, but this time around, he said that I should mind my own business. That if I didn't, he couldn't guarantee what would happen."

He froze. Anger surged inside him. "Are you just now telling me that Eric *threatened* you?"

She seemed nonplussed. "Yes…?"

He swore. "That's something you lead with, Graciela! Jesus Christ, what if he'd done something to you? Were you alone? Of course you were. My God, that little piece of shit…"

"I'm fine." She grabbed his arm. "He didn't hurt me. He just wanted to scare me away."

Jaime growled. "This isn't helping."

"Fine, but don't dismiss everything I've said, okay? I think if we delve deeper, we can prove that Eric set you up. That he's the one stealing from River's Bend."

He knew she was about to say this, but it sounded so absurd that he barked out a laugh. "Eric O'Neill isn't remotely smart enough to do something like this."

"Maybe, maybe not. But maybe he has help."

He could see she wasn't going to back down. He sighed, taking her hand. He wanted to burn something down—preferably Eric's place—at the thought of him threatening her. But at the same time, another emotion pierced through the darkness: gratitude. And awe. Both because this woman put herself on the line to find out the truth.

He pulled her into an embrace. "Thank you," he said. He couldn't say anything more.

"I'd do anything for you."

He just held her tighter, his heart about to burst from his chest.

He didn't deserve her. Burying his face into her hair, he knew this with a clarity that tore at his soul.

CHAPTER FIFTEEN

Although Grace would've preferred to stay at Joy's for the foreseeable future, she knew she couldn't avoid her parents forever. She also needed clean clothes. Thus, she made her way back home, wondering if she could sneak inside without anyone noticing.

Seeing not only her parents' car, but Adam's car—and another one with a Massachusetts license plate, which she knew was Gavin's—she had a feeling she wasn't going to be able to sneak around anytime soon. She took a deep breath. Might as well get this over with.

When she went inside, she first went into the kitchen, but found no one. It was eerily quiet. She glanced upstairs before she walked into the living room. Seeing her entire family sitting there, she stopped in her tracks.

Her mom and dad sat on one couch, while Adam and Joy sat on the other. Gavin with his young daughter Emma sat on a chair, and Grace thought Gavin looked particularly uncomfortable. He'd just arrived in Heron's Landing with Emma last night, but Grace had been so preoccupied that she'd honestly forgotten all about it.

"Gavin," she said, choosing to ignore everyone else. "Emma!" She embraced the little girl, who didn't hug her back. She drew back into her dad's embrace, like she didn't know how to take having her aunt standing in front of her.

Gavin whispered something in Emma's ear. She stood up, and then he embraced Grace.

"Nice to see you, sis." He pulled back to look at her. "How are you?"

She rather felt like crying. It might've been because Gavin looked older and tired, and she could detect silver strands in his dark hair. When they were younger, he and Adam had often been mistaken for twins even though there was two years between them. Now she thought that Gavin looked older. She wanted to ask him about Teagan, about Emma, about himself, but she could feel the stares of the rest of the family on her back.

She forced a smile. "I'm all right. I'm glad you're here."

He gave her a lopsided smile, but only patted her on the arm. Emma sat down on the ottoman in front of the chair, her face decidedly blank. She had white blonde hair and the biggest blue eyes Grace had ever seen. She also had an uncanny knack to sit and watch people without saying a word. Grace hadn't seen her niece much since Gavin and Teagan had been living in Boston, but she hoped she could get to know her, now that they were in Heron's Landing.

She heard someone clear their throat. Turning, Grace looked at each person in the living room, almost daring them to say something.

"Grace, dear, why don't you sit down?" Julia beckoned to her to sit on the couch next to her.

Grace almost said no, but at her mother's look, she decided not to fight. Sitting down gingerly, she asked, "Are we having a meeting of some sort? Because I have to tell you, I didn't get an invitation."

She could see Joy looking like she wanted to say something, while Adam looked like he had a dark cloud hovering over his head. Grace didn't want to look at her father. She knew he was glowering at her.

"We're glad you came home," Julia began, touching Grace's knee. "We wanted to talk to you about something."

"I feel like it's time for me to say that I did not agree to this," Joy said. She gave Adam a look, and he gave her a "we'll discuss this later" expression.

"Thank you," Grace replied. "I think?"

"This is ridiculous. Just cut to the chase, will you?" Carl practically growled. "Young lady, you should know that your behavior as of late has been atrocious. You've completely disregarded basic decency, and to top it off, have decided that spending your time with a criminal is in your best interests."

"Jaime is not a criminal!" She glared at her father, who was about to open his mouth again when Julia shushed him. "Why are all of you so insistent on making him out to be a bad guy? He didn't do anything wrong."

She was about to storm off, but Julia took her hand. "We know, dear," she said soothingly. "Please just listen, all right?"

Grace bit her lip and nodded.

Adam leaned forward, and his expression was so stormy, so full of roiling emotions that Grace could barely look at him. "I was informed this morning by Sheriff Jennings that they are pressing charges against Jaime. Once the paperwork is done, he'll be placed under arrest."

Grace stared at him. "Why...how...?"

Her throat closed. This couldn't be happening. Jaime didn't deserve this.

"They've found sufficient evidence, as far as I understand it. I know it's not what you wanted to hear," Julia said. "None of us wanted to hear that Jaime would do something like this."

She pulled her arm away from her mother. "Don't. Don't act like you care. Don't act like you haven't been convinced he was guilty since the second the money went missing." She didn't know if she wanted to scream or cry more. She looked at everyone sitting here, even at Gavin, who had nothing to do with any of this. She looked at Joy, who gave her a look full of sympathy.

Grace couldn't breathe. She had to warn Jaime.

"When are they arresting him?" she asked, because she needed to know how much time she had.

Adam shrugged. "They didn't tell me. I just know it's soon. It could be today, it could be in a week."

"And that's it? He's going to jail and we'll just sit here and act like it doesn't matter?" Grace breathed, but it came out more like a sob. "We'll let it go and act like we never cared about him at all?"

"Of course not. Adam is working to make sure Jaime doesn't go to jail for a long time. He doesn't even want to press charges," Julia said.

Grace laughed. Tears blurred her vision, and she laughed and laughed. She knew her family was looking at her like she'd lost her mind. Maybe she had. Maybe she'd gone crazy the second she'd laid eyes on Jaime, all those years ago.

"Honey…" Julia reached out to touch her again.

"No!" Grace pulled away and stood up. "Don't you dare." She wiped her eyes, remembering the receipts, the checks. She grabbed her bag and began furiously rifling through it. She heard someone say her name, but she didn't care. She tossed the papers on the coffee table and kneeling down, began sorting through them.

"Look, I've found all of these invoices. They show gradual price increases for almost all of the items, and for ones that shouldn't have become more expensive."

She handed the invoices to Adam. He didn't say anything, and he didn't ask if she'd been in his office. He glanced at them. Then he handed them back, shaking his head. "Grace, this doesn't prove anything."

She wanted to scream. She shoved the checks toward him. "Look at these then! You're missing checks, Adam. And I can tell you right now that it wasn't Jaime who stole that money. It was Eric. Eric's the one who's been stealing right under your nose and setting Jaime up to take the fall."

No one said anything. You could hear a pin drop, it was so silent. Grace sat on the floor, trembling with rage and despair.

When she looked up, though, she saw that Adam's jaw was rigid. Her heart fell. He didn't believe her. She looked at her mother, and Julia just shook her head. Even Joy didn't say anything.

"Grace, the police have found enough evidence to charge Jaime. If Eric had been responsible, don't you think they would've realized that?" Adam implored her, his dark eyebrows furrowed.

Grace couldn't move. She couldn't breathe. It was like

someone was burying her alive, shoveling soil on top of her until she suffocated. It was all she could do not to panic.

But reaching deep down inside herself, she found the strength to stand up and collect the papers she'd strewn across the living room. She bit back the tears pushing at her eyelids, her hands trembling and her heart pounding. When she looked behind her, she saw Emma staring at her, her blue eyes wide with confusion.

Clutching her bag, she said in a low voice, "I know Jaime is innocent. He is one of the best men I've ever met. He is good, and kind, and he's my friend." Her voice stuttered on *friend*, because he was so much more than that. "I'm not going to sit here and condemn him because none of you are capable of looking beyond the obvious."

Carl stood up as well, pointing a finger at her. "If you go out that door to go to him, young lady, just know that we will not let you back into this house. That's my final warning. I've had enough of this behavior."

"Carl!" Julia exclaimed.

Grace laughed, but it was a sad, devastating laugh. She slung her bag over her shoulder. "Then I guess this is good-bye." She looked at Emma and Gavin, the latter of whom was looking both shocked and bemused.

"Grace..." Gavin said.

She nodded at him and Emma and then, without looking at anyone else, she left. She drove her car to Jaime's because she had to warn him. She knew he couldn't go anywhere. She knew that if they were pressing charges, nothing she could say or do would help. But he deserved to know. The tears from before dried up, and she was only filled with desperation and a need to see him. This one last time.

But as she pulled up into his driveway, she saw that she was too late. Three cop cars were outside his house—which she had to admit was rather excessive. She ran to his front door and burst through the open door, only to see Jaime in his living room with four cops surrounding him.

"Jaime Martínez, you are under arrest," Sheriff Jennings said as another cop cuffed him. "Anything you say can be used against you in a court of law."

One cop who Grace didn't recognize raised his eyebrows at her presence. "Ma'am, you can't be here." He moved to escort her out.

But she didn't move. Jaime wouldn't look at her. She wanted to beg him to look at her, so she could tell him she was here to warn him even though it was too late. When the cop touched her arm, she pulled away.

"Ma'am, please. If you don't cooperate, we'll have to take you in, too."

She trembled, saying nothing. But eventually she nodded. The officer took her outside, but when she asked to stay by her car, he seemed to take pity on her and let her stay.

She watched as the three other cops brought Jaime out of his house, his hands behind his back and his gaze on the ground. He still wouldn't look at her. The tears that had disappeared returned, and she let them fall unimpeded. This wasn't right. This couldn't be happening, yet no matter how hard she'd tried, it had all been for nothing.

Sheriff Jennings placed Jaime in the back of a cop car, shutting the door. All but the officer who'd escorted Grace from the house went back inside. Sensing this was her only opportunity, she walked up to the officer; she read his nametag: HALDON.

Officer Haldon was fairly young, perhaps not much older than Grace, with surprisingly kind eyes and a look about him that seemed to hint he hadn't been on the force for long. When he saw Grace approach him, though, he narrowed his eyes.

"Ma'am, please step away from the suspect."

She stopped, but in a pleading voice, said, "May I just talk to him? Say goodbye? Please. I'll leave and never bother you again."

Officer Haldon considered. She knew he saw the tears on her face, and how desperate she sounded. She also knew that he'd probably assume that a young woman like her couldn't be any real threat. He glanced back at the house, then back at her. "Three minutes," he said. "You can sit on the passenger side. But if you do anything suspicious, you'll be going to the same place as him."

She nodded. "Thank you."

Officer Haldon opened the passenger front door, and then Grace slipped inside. The officer stood right next to the door with Grace in his line of vision and with the window cracked so he could hear their conversation. But she didn't care. She turned and saw Jaime through the mesh that separated the front seat from the back.

Jaime stared at his feet. She could only see that his expression was grim, his mouth in a thin line.

"Jaime. Jaime, look at me."

He clenched his jaw. Then he looked up at her, and his eyes were such a mixture of defeat and sadness and shame that her tears started all over again.

"I wanted to tell you. I wanted to warn you. That's why I'm

here." She was babbling, making no sense. "I had no idea this was going to happen."

The hardness in his face softened some. "How could you have known? It's not your fault."

"No, no, don't be kind to me." She cried harder. "You're the one who needs people to be kind. You shouldn't be here. This is wrong." She wiped her eyes, but the tears wouldn't stop. "I know you're innocent."

"Hush, Graciela." He leaned toward the mesh, his forehead almost touching it. "You can't do anything, at least not right now." His gaze intensified, like he could impart what he really wanted to say in that look. "But we both know this isn't the end. Right?"

She nodded. "Yes, of course." She pressed her fingers into the mesh, touching his cheek. She knew she was probably overstepping her bounds, but she didn't care. She didn't care if they threw her in jail, too. "I have some savings. I can use that as bail."

He shook his head. She could see him still clenching his jaw, and through her haze of tears, she saw the shimmer of tears in his eyes. She touched his bottom lip, and her heart broke when he kissed it. Just a brush of his lips. But it was enough—for now.

"You're killing me," he said simply, devastatingly. "I don't deserve you."

"Don't say that. You've been nothing but kind to me. You were my first, in so many ways." When she saw Officer Haldon giving her a look to knock it off, she pulled away from Jaime. But she didn't stop speaking. "I love you," she said in a soft voice.

Jaime didn't say anything, but he seemed to breathe harder. She saw a tear track down his face.

"I love you," she repeated. "And I'm going to do everything I can to get you out of this."

He swallowed and she heard him say her name. She was about to reach out to touch him when the passenger door opened.

"Okay, time's up," Officer Haldon said. "We're taking him in."

Grace stepped out. "Where are you taking him?" Heron's Landing was too small to have its own holding cells.

"We'll take him up to Columbia. We'll book him and set bail. You can call up there for updates if you want."

She nodded. She watched as Sheriff Jennings got into the car and she stepped away. The car drove off with the other two officers following close behind. Officer Haldon stayed standing next to her, and she had a feeling he almost wanted to touch her shoulder in sympathy. But he just cleared his throat and asked in a gruff voice, "You'll be okay, ma'am?"

She almost laughed. "I'll be fine. I'm not the one who you should be worrying about." Before she turned to leave, she added, "Thank you for letting me talk to him."

He nodded tightly before also driving off.

Grace stood there, feeling the world turn to twilight. It was cold, and she was—as usual—not wearing a coat. She went inside Jaime's house and locked the door before lying down on the couch. She inhaled his scent, rubbing her cheek against the fabric, and she let the tears flow. She cried and cried, not even sure how much time passed. All she knew was that heart was broken, and she wasn't sure how she'd ever be happy again.

Much later, she got a text. Then another. When she got a third, she took her phone from her bag and scanned the words on her phone. It was from Joy.

I heard what happened. Are you at Jaime's? We're worried about you. Do you want to stay with me?

Then: *Grace, please answer.*

Then: *I'm coming over.*

It was only a few minutes later that Grace heard a car door slam. Joy entered and Grace simply lay on the couch, like she were paralyzed.

"Oh, Grace." Joy squatted down next to her and brushed her hair from her face. "We're going to my place, okay?"

She bit her lip and then, before she could stop herself, she threw her arms around Joy's neck and sobbed into her shoulder.

CHAPTER SIXTEEN

Jaime stared down at the concrete floor of his holding cell and watched as a spider scurried into a corner. The spider—some little brown thing with more legs than sense—crawled up the wall, to hang in a web it'd created between the cell door and the wall.

He wondered if this was a metaphor for his life. He'd gotten caught in a web, or maybe he was the spider stupid enough to create a web in a jail cell. He closed his eyes. He wished he could sleep, but the thought of closing his eyes in this place was unbearable.

So he stared at the spider and watched it rebuild a hole in its web instead of thinking about everything that had happened that day.

Of course, it was impossible not to think about what had happened. The knock on his door, the officers pouring in, the cold bite of cuffs on his wrists. That had been bad enough. But then Grace had shown up and seen him like that, and it had taken all of his strength not to beg her to leave. He couldn't bear for her to see him as some criminal. It didn't matter that he was innocent: that had been lowest point of his life.

He'd known she wouldn't abandon him. Not his Graciela. No, she'd somehow sweet-talked one of the cops into letting her talk to him in the car. Her voice had soothed his agitation. While half of him wanted her gone, the other half had almost cried with relief that she was there.

Seeing her tears and hearing her promises had wrecked him—more than the cuffs biting into his wrists or the charges laid against him. He knew she'd fight for him until her dying breath. And because Grace was Grace, she'd told him she loved him *again* and he was fairly certain if her goal was to destroy him, she'd done it without laying a hand on him.

The hours petered on. The spider seemed to have taken a nap—if spiders even slept—and now the only movement in the room was Jaime's fingers tapping against his knee. It was stupid, but the drumming reminded himself that he was still alive. He wasn't really sure otherwise.

Although he wanted to get out of this place, he also knew that he had nowhere to go. He couldn't return to Heron's Landing; his job was as good as gone. He didn't know if he could get another job as a chef. Who was he except a chef? He'd poured his life into becoming the best, and now it had all been swept away within a day. Within hours.

Jaime balled his fist against his leg. If before he had only felt despair, now he felt rage. He raged against Eric doing this to him, he raged against Adam for not believing in him, he raged against the police for using flimsy evidence to book him, and he even raged against Grace for believing that they could do something to prevent this from happening. He realized he was gasping for air, almost hyperventilating, but the swirl of anger didn't dissipate. Instead, it felt like it grew into every crevice of his being until that was all he was. A being of unadulterated rage.

He didn't know what time it was when he heard a lock clicking. The door swung open, and the young cop who'd let Grace talk to him stepped in; Office Haldon was his name. "You can have your one phone call now, Mr. Martínez. Do you know who that'll be?"

Jaime stared at the man. Who could he call? His parents? The thought of their devastation on his behalf made him grimace. Grace couldn't help him; neither could Adam. So he just shook his head.

Office Haldon gazed at him before sighing. "Well, let me know if you think of someone. You need anything? A bottle of water?"

Jaime shook his head, a meager movement. "I'm fine," he said in a low voice.

"Okay, well, let me know."

The officer locked him up again. Jaime waited. He didn't know what he was waiting for. Was he going to sit in this cell for the rest of his life? He closed his eyes again. God, he was tired. So tired. Maybe if he just took a quick nap, he could figure out what the hell he wanted to do…

He must've fallen asleep, because the next thing Jaime knew Officer Haldon was shaking him awake. "Hey, someone's here to bail you out."

Jaime blinked. He stared at the officer's face, noticed that he had a mole on his left eyebrow, and then the words finally registered. *Someone, bail, you.* "What?" Jaime croaked.

"You've been bailed out. Come on, you don't want to stay here." The officer shook him again, and Jaime stood up, his joints creaky from falling asleep on the bench. He looked up and saw that the spider had disappeared, which for some reason made him smile.

Office Haldon escorted him out of the cell area, and after going through the locked doors, Jaime stopped in his tracks when he saw who was waiting for him.

It was Adam.

"Jaime." Adam came toward him and embraced him, slapping him on the back. "Jesus Christ, what a mess this is."

Jaime didn't hug him back. He didn't know how to feel about any of this.

"We need to finish some paperwork," Office Haldon said, "and then you can go. We'll also mail you information regarding your court date."

Jaime stepped away from Adam. Filling out so many pieces of paper that his vision blurred, he was shocked to see that it was early morning when he and Adam walked outside. The sky was streaked with orange and purple, and when they breathed, it hung in a cloud in front of them. An owl hooted from nearby.

"Let's go get some coffee and talk. It's fucking freezing." Adam walked down the sidewalk, and Jaime followed him, mostly because he had no ride back home.

Back home. Was Heron's Landing even his home anymore?

They walked the streets of downtown Columbia, which were deserted. The students at the nearby University of Missouri had all gone home for winter break, and as it was too early for anyone else to be around, it felt like a ghost town. Adam took Jaime to a coffee shop that had a grand total of one person inside, making drinks. Probably a college student who didn't have the money to travel home, Jaime thought.

After getting two large mugs of black coffee and a few pastries, the two men sat at a table in the back. Jaime wrapped his hands around the mug, only just noticing how cold he was. Adam looked at him and then, without a word, went and got him a large glass of water, which he pushed toward him with another look.

Jaime gulped the water. It helped. Adam pushed a croissant toward him, which he ate with gusto. He realized he hadn't eaten for almost twelve hours.

Now feeling slightly more human, Jaime sipped his coffee and stared at his friend and boss from across the table. The boss who had betrayed him, and the friend who had bailed him out. He couldn't find any words to say, so he sipped his coffee and waited.

"How are you?" Adam asked, tearing a Danish into tiny pieces.

Jaime just drank his coffee. "I'm fucking exhausted," he muttered.

"I'm sure." Adam kept tearing at the Danish; he hadn't touched his coffee. "Look, Jaime…"

Jaime put up a hand. "I'm too tired to hear your excuses."

"I don't have excuses, just explanations." At Jaime's look, Adam sighed. "I didn't press charges. Sheriff Jennings did. I'll admit I wasn't sure what to think when it happened."

"You thought I was guilty."

When Adam didn't say anything, Jaime had his answer. The coffee turned sour in his stomach. He'd thought as much, but there was nothing like having it confirmed.

"I'll be honest: I thought you were guilty for about a day."

Adam clutched his mug of coffee, having given up on the Danish. "But then I thought about it, and I knew you couldn't be. And then Grace basically ripped my head off and showed me all of the receipts and checks she'd found in my office..."

Jaime stilled. Grace had confronted her family—for him?

"What did Grace tell you?" Jaime stared at the inside of his mug.

"If you mean, did she tell us about what's going on between you two? She said nothing. But she's been looking for evidence to prove your innocence for weeks. She came to my place after you'd been arrested and gave me an earful. She said that if I didn't bail you out she'd never speak to me again and probably poison my water supply."

Jaime smiled a little. "She would, too."

"But although the threat of poisoning was concerning, it wasn't why I bailed you out."

Looking up, Jaime saw his friend smiling sadly.

"I did it because I know you're innocent. I did it because I should've worked harder to keep you out of this mess. I did it because I'm sorrier than I can ever explain—for all of this."

When Adam said *all of this,* Jaime had a feeling he meant not only the stolen money, but also his demand to stay away from Grace. Torn between anger that it'd taken Adam this long to realize this and relief that his friend believed in him, Jaime said nothing. He didn't know what to say about anything anymore.

"I also want you to know that I'll help any way I can, with lawyers and everything." Adam's brow furrowed, like he wasn't sure if Jaime were listening. "And your job at River's Bend is still waiting for you, too."

Jaime had the sudden wish to see Grace. To hear her voice.

To have her arms around him. To bury his face in that long blonde hair. She could make him feel like a person again.

He cleared his throat. "Thanks," he said. It was all he could say at this point.

Adam nodded, like he understood.

They finished their coffee and drove back to Heron's Landing, saying little on the way there. Jaime didn't know if they could ever be close friends again. It was difficult to trust someone who had lost their trust in you, even if it had only been for a day. But he was also so exhausted he could barely think straight. He just needed to go home, he needed to sleep, he needed to call his parents. He knew Adam would let him have his job back, but he didn't want it anymore. To return to the vineyard, to have his coworkers judging him, always thinking he was going to steal again? To have Chris look at him like a criminal, to have Eric sneer at him?

He'd rather cut his arm off than go back there.

After Adam had dropped Jaime off at his house, Jaime sat in his living room, not knowing how to move. How to think. How to *be*. It was the strangest feeling. It was like he couldn't recognize anything in his house. The couch, the photos, the plates on the counter, the leftover food in the fridge—none of it was his. It didn't even smell the same. How did that happen? He hadn't been gone for longer than day.

As morning passed into afternoon, Jaime got up and took a shower. He threw out the clothes he'd worn to jail. He saw the papers from the police station and it was like something switched inside of him. His exhaustion melted away until only that rage he'd felt inside his cell took over again. His vision turned red, his fists clenched, and he watched himself—like he'd been separated from his body—kneel onto the ground, his head in his hands. A scream tried to escape from his throat, but nothing came out.

He had to get out of here. He put on his tennis shoes and jacket and made his way down to the river, the same spot he'd found Grace all those weeks ago. But when he got there, it was just him and the river, and he was glad of it. He shouted and swore and threw rocks into the water, pacing and swearing and letting all of the blackness pour out of him. It was cathartic; it was exhausting. If he thought about how he was behaving, he'd probably be embarrassed. But it felt good. He exorcised the sharpest corners of his rage until his emotions muted, until he felt drained but relieved.

He collapsed on the riverbank, breathing hard. He laughed a little. He was probably hysterical. He imagined Grace seeing him, telling him he was an idiot. He *was* an idiot. The biggest idiot in the universe, to fall in love with a girl he'd told himself he couldn't have.

Jaime stayed at the river, staring at the water flowing by. Many of the usual birds had flown south for the winter, so it was just crows squalling in the trees. After a while, Jaime started to shiver from the cold. He knew he couldn't sit here forever, even if he wished that he could.

Returning home, he stripped out of his dirty clothes and began packing. Before that, though, he called his parents and told them what had happened. His mother cried while his father had barely spoken, but Jaime assured them that he would get this figured out. He knew he didn't sound convinced, but his parents didn't argue. Instead, they pressed him to come home, and he agreed. He needed to go home. It didn't matter that he was almost thirty years old: sometimes you just needed to go home to your parents when your heart was broken.

Jaime stuffed clothes into his suitcase, snagging shoes and random toiletries. Did it even matter what he took? It all felt so pointless now. He still didn't have his laptop, so he'd have to use his parents' ancient desktop for the time being. Luckily, most of his files were in the cloud, so he could access his resume and start applying for jobs.

He knew, though, that he was avoiding what he had to do before leaving. He had to see Grace. He ached to see her, to hold her, although the thought of saying goodbye made him freeze in his tracks.

He texted her, asking her where she was staying. Her response was immediate. *I'm at Joy's again. Are you okay? Adam told me he'd gotten you out and I wanted to come see you, but I thought you might need some time alone.*

How did she know him so well? He shook his head, sighing. *I'll be over in a little bit, if Joy doesn't mind.*

She says it's fine. She says she can go over to Adam's for the night.

Jaime drove over to Joy's, parking outside. He saw Mike come out of the general store, and the older man just raised his eyebrows at Jaime's appearance. He was sure the whole town knew of his arrest and subsequent release. But at this point, he didn't care.

Joy opened the door when he arrived. She looked tired, but relieved.

"You look terrible," she said. "Let me get you something to drink. Grace, Jaime's here."

Grace came out, and she looked as tired as he felt. She went to him, hugging him tightly, and he did the same. He hugged her so hard that she made a squeaky sound, but she didn't tell him to stop.

Joy put a hand on his arm. "You guys talk. I'm going over to Adam's. Feel free to eat whatever you want. I'm glad you're back, by the way."

"Thanks, Joy," Jaime said.

She nodded, grabbing her purse and coat and closing the door quietly behind her.

He and Grace stood there, their arms wrapped around each other. He heard a sniffle, and he realized that she was crying.

He tipped her head back. "Please don't cry," he urged. "I can't stand it."

"How can I not cry? All of this—I can't…"

He pulled her closer, until it was like their bodies were completely entwined. She cried, and he cried, and then she looked up at him with those eyes.

She kissed him, and it was like coming home again.

CHAPTER SEVENTEEN

Grace knew they needed to talk about what had happened. She needed to know what had happened to him in the past twenty-four hours, as she'd been imagining all sorts of terrible things. She only knew that Jaime had been arrested and that Adam had bailed him out. And now he was here, with her, and kissing her like it was the last time he'd ever see her.

She didn't want this to be the end. So she clung to him, like she was ivy encircling him, the stoic oak tree who could shelter her from the harshest elements.

They didn't make it to the bedroom. Jaime picked her up and she wrapped her legs around his waist as he carried her to the living room couch. He sat down with her with her in his lap, and she could feel his hardness through their dual layer of jeans. She ran her fingers through his hair; his day's worth of stubble scratched at her cheeks and lips, but she didn't care.

His hands trailed up her belly. She gasped as his fingers cupped her breast through her bra. Still kissing her, they both groaned as he played with her, plucking at her nipple, making her squirm against him. Clothes suddenly seemed completely unnecessary. Drawing back, she lifted her shirt over her head, her hair tumbling down to her waist. She was about to put it up so it wouldn't get in the way, but Jaime stopped her.

"I want to see it down." He reached to run his fingers through its strands, touching her skin as he did so. "I want to see you naked with your hair down as you ride me."

His words sparked something inside of her. She kissed him, gripping his shoulders. He reached behind her and unclasped her bra. She shucked off her jeans and panties, and he unbuckled his belt. Unzipping his jeans, she pulled his cock free, and he groaned as she stroked him.

Grace couldn't help but marvel that this man wanted her. She couldn't believe she was here, with his hands all over her, his breath mingling with her own, his cock in her hand. He palmed her ass as she fondled him, and it only made her desire increase. His clever fingers trailed down until he parted her folds, feeling how wet she was.

She rubbed against him. If he just went slightly higher, she knew she'd come. She was already that close. She made a humming noise in the back of her throat, but Jaime just kept playing with her, only making her crazier.

When his thumb brushed her clit, she shuddered. "I'm not going to last much longer," she moaned.

He kissed her breast. "Then don't." He rubbed that thumb of his again, and she went off. She gave a long moan and felt her entire body tremble. She had to lean forward and grip his shoulders to keep her balance. She melted; her bones turned to jelly. Gasping and moaning, she felt Jaime grip her hip with one hand as his other hand continued to touch her with feather-light brushes.

Grace needed him inside of her, but when he reached inside his back pocket to unfold his wallet, she was momentarily confused. As he plucked a condom from the wallet's depths, she laughed.

"You're prepared." She took the foil packet and ripped it open before smoothing the latex down his cock.

He hitched his hips as she touched his cock. "I thought it'd be rude to keep stealing Joy's."

But all words were lost when she felt him probe at her entrance, so hot and hard. He held her hips again, but told her to take control. She felt for his cock and slowly descended upon it, feeling every inch of him as he stretched her. It didn't hurt, but she felt full, almost overwhelmed. Breathing in pants, she moved until he was inside of her completely, her ass against his jean-covered thighs.

"Jesus Christ," he muttered, tangling his fingers in her hair as he kissed her. "Fuck, you feel amazing."

She shuddered. She moved her hair over to one shoulder, and it brushed her nipples as she began to ride him. Beginning with shallow strokes, she worked him, not wanting this to be over too soon. He clutched at her hips, almost painfully so, but it only egged her on. Soon her rhythm increased until the sounds of their bodies coming together filled the room. From then on, it was only gasps and moans and exclamations of *right there* and *yes, God, yes*. Grace could feel her body spiraling again, could feel herself clenching around his cock, and when he leaned her forward he hit a new spot that made her pant.

They stared into each other's eyes as their bodies climbed upward, and it was the most erotic thing Grace had ever experienced. Watching Jaime's eyes darken, his cheeks slightly flushed, his mouth open, his hair falling across his forehead.

The way his hands held her hips and brought her up and down as she rode him, how his cock reached places inside of her she never imagined existed. She breathed his name just as her body shattered, her hair a curtain around them. She heard him say something, but it was lost in the ecstasy of the moment.

She vaguely heard him shout. Then his body shook, and they kissed, teeth and tongues tangling; it was messy and almost savage but Grace didn't care. She didn't care if she ended up bloodied and bruised. It would only serve to remind her of everything that had happened with this man underneath her.

But reality soon returned to the both of them. Grace got dressed again and Jaime put his shirt back on, and they spooned together on the couch. She stroked his arm, feeling his heart pound against her back. She suddenly wished she could sleep forever.

"Can you tell me what happened?" she whispered, concentrating on the dark hair scattered across his wrist and forearm.

She felt him shift and sigh. His leg brushed against hers. Finally, he told her about getting booked, about sitting in the jail cell, about how Adam bailed him out. His voice took on a deadened quality, and she could tell there was more to it than he was saying. She wondered what he thought about, sitting there, not knowing what would happen next. She stroked his arm, as if she could soothe the pain away with her fingers.

She brought his arm between her breasts, cradling it. He pressed his face against her, muffling his voice. She didn't know what he was saying or if he were saying anything at all. But she felt his body tremble, and she knew that she'd keep him, close to her heart, for as long as it took to bring him back to himself.

"But they're still pressing charges?" Grace turned around to see his face now.

He brushed his fingers across her forehead. "As far as I know. They just let me out on bail. I'll still have a court date." He huffed out a breath. "I think it's time I get a lawyer. Even though I'm not sure how I'll afford a decent one."

"But we can work to find more evidence, right? We're so close. We both know it was Eric who set you up."

Jaime didn't say anything. He just touched her lightly, like he was memorizing her shape. "I don't think that's a good idea," he admitted.

"Why not? Who else is going to do it but us?"

"You keep saying *us*. Graciela, I can't let you keep doing this." He stroked her cheek. "You're at odds with your family because of this. Because of *me*. And who knows what Eric will do. He's a wild card. I'm not going to put you in danger for me."

She stared at him. Was he really giving up? "I'm not just going to let you rot in jail."

"I know that, and I'm grateful for your help. But I'm also know that if you push further, something is going to happen."

She was about to tell him he was overreacting, but at the look on his face, she bit her cheek instead. She didn't feel like she was in any danger, and her family could go rot. This was about him, not anyone else.

At her stubborn expression, he pressed her fingers. "Don't do anything else. Please. For me? This is my battle, not yours."

Her heart sunk, but she nodded tightly. The thought of giving up when they were so close ate at her. But Jaime's relieved sigh showed her that in this way, she could take off at least one of the many burdens on his shoulders.

And at any rate, she could keep working without him ever knowing about it.

~

JAIME LEFT to go home shortly thereafter. Although Grace had asked what he was going to do, he'd just shaken his head and kissed her goodbye. She didn't know what that meant. Was he staying here? She didn't want him to leave, of course, but at the same time, she'd have a difficult time staying in a place that had thought so poorly of her.

The thought was too depressing, though. Leaving Joy's to get some fresh air, Grace wandered down Main Street, running into a few locals but for the most part, keeping to herself. The day was cold, and as she walked by the buildings and saw all of the Christmas lights and trees decorated in the windows, she realized that Christmas was only a week away. How had that happened?

She stood in front of the local antiques shop, where they'd put up a bright silver tree covered in pink lights and ornaments. The shop owner, Dotty, had a thing for pink. The entire window had spots of pink: a pink tree skirt adorned the bottom of the tree, and was that pink cotton snow underneath? For some reason, the bright lights of the tree and the vague sound of Christmas music brought tears to her eyes.

The weight of the world fell upon her shoulders. She didn't know who to turn to anymore. Her parents had decided she wasn't worth the trouble, and Adam was too overwhelmed with the vineyard and with his own life. Joy had been there for her, but even Joy had her limits. And now Jaime was probably leaving Heron's Landing. Where did she fit in all of this?

She walked away. She went down to the creek, which had long frozen over. Tying her scarf tighter about her throat, Grace sat down on a log and stared at the bare trees. Her mind emptied of everything. A kind of peace settled on her at last, and she took a deep breath, hoping she could hold onto it as long as possible.

It wasn't meant to be, though. She heard footsteps behind her, and when she turned, her eyes widened when she saw that it was Eric of all people. She'd never seen him walking around Heron's Landing, let alone come down to this creek. He didn't seem particularly interested in something as boring as *nature.*

She didn't have anything to say to him. She turned away without greeting him, hoping that he'd get the hint and move on. But she didn't have that kind of luck. He sat down at the other end of the log, like he planned to stay there for a while.

Grace glared at him. Fine. If he was going to invade her space, then she'd go somewhere else.

"Wait," he said. "I need to talk to you."

She turned, and remaining standing, waited. Eric didn't seem nervous or like he was going to apologize. He seemed irritated, his mouth in a harsh line.

"What is it?" Grace asked.

He didn't stand up, but his scowl turned into a smile, which made Grace's blood turn cold. He leaned forward, his forearms on his thighs.

"I think you know what this is about," is all he said.

She willed her pounding heart to calm. He didn't know anything. He was bluffing.

"If you came here to talk in riddles, then I'm leaving." She turned to leave.

"I know that you've found the invoices," he called. "I know you've been sniffing around things you shouldn't be."

She needed to go. She walked five quick steps when a hand latched onto her elbow, pulling her back. She yelped.

"I told you to leave things alone, but you didn't listen, did you?" his voice hissed in her ear. "You thought you'd help your boyfriend out, but all you've done is make things worse for him."

Grace struggled, but Eric was taller and bigger than her, and his grip held firm. His fingers dug into her elbow so hard that she had to stifle a cry.

"What do you want?" she asked.

"I want you to leave things alone." He scowled, yanking her toward him. "But it's too late for that, isn't it? If you would've listened to me, this wouldn't have to happen."

Fear coursed through her until she knew she was shaking like a rabbit. She realized she was all alone with this man, this man who'd frame his boss without an ounce of regret, and she opened her mouth to scream.

Eric covered her mouth before she let out more than a yelp. "If you scream," he said as he pulled her against him, her back to his front, "you'll regret it."

She didn't know what he was going to do. Was he going to kill her? Rape her? Both? Panic hit her, and she started struggling. It was all elbows and hands and fingers and she could barely tell who was who. She let out a short scream, but it was stifled when he backhanded her across the face.

Grace collapsed. Breathing hard, she tried to will away the dizziness from his slap. Her cheek smarted, and tears stung her eyes. He crouched next to her and yanked her head back by her hair.

"I told you to leave it alone." He pulled so hard that she gasped.

After that, Grace just knew she had to fight. She had to get his hands off of her, she had to get away. She felt dirt underneath her palms and she fell against a rock that cut her knee, even under the layer of her jeans. She gasped and when Eric was about to hit her again, she screamed so loudly that surely the trees shook.

For that, he was about to backhand her again. But before his hand connected with her face, Grace heard what she could only describe as an inhuman roar and then flesh pounded against flesh.

She staggered upward. She watched, in a daze, as Jaime punched Eric in the nose. The two men struggled, with Eric falling to the ground and Jaime kicking him in the ribs. Eric groaned and started begging and pleading, but it was like Jaime was deaf to the world.

Grace could barely understand what was happening, but she knew if Jaime kept this up something irrevocable could happen. She flew to him, grasping his arm, telling him to stop. "You'll kill him," she heard someone say, only realizing later that she was saying it. "You'll kill him. Stop. Stop!"

Jaime jerked away from her. He gasped for air, swearing and looking like he could strangle Eric with his bare hands. Eric lay on the ground still as he groaned, clutching his ribs. Stepping toward Eric, Jaime stood over him and said in a voice that lifted the hairs on the back of Grace's neck, "If you ever come near Grace again, I'll kill you. Do you hear me? I don't care what happens to me. If you touch her—if you *breathe* near her—you're done for."

Eric swore but when Jaime looked like he could hit him again, he finally nodded.

"Let's go." Jaime steered Grace away and she found herself in his truck. She only stared as he asked her what happened, where did Eric touch her, *Jesus Christ, Grace, say something.*

She blinked. She felt wetness on her cheeks, and she realized she was crying.

When Jaime embraced her, she broke. She started crying in gasping sobs, the terror of the moment making her unable to speak. She could barely breathe. Jaime rubbed her back, assuring her that he'd keep her safe. He held her close, and she burrowed into his arms.

She never wanted to leave his arms.

After some time, he examined her face, tracing her bruised cheek. His expression became murderous once again.

"I'll kill him," he said in a low voice.

Grace hissed at the pain of him just brushing her cheek. "And then you'll go to jail for the rest of your life," she replied.

"It would be worth it."

"And leave me all alone?" She laid her head on his shoulder, and he caressed her hair. She clung to his arm. "How did you find me?" she asked softly.

"I came to see you, but Mike said he'd seen you go out for a walk. Then I heard something in the woods, and then you screamed…" He kissed the top of her head. "I'm so sorry this happened."

"It wasn't your fault." She looked up, but she could see in

his face that he blamed himself. "It wasn't. It was Eric. He attacked me."

But Jaime was shaking his head. "It wouldn't have happened if not for me. Let me shoulder the guilt, okay? I deserve it."

She wanted to argue with him. She wanted to shake him and make him see sense. But she was too tired. Her cheek hurt and she just wanted to go home. Jaime gently let her go and drove her back to Joy's, where he made an ice pack for her cheek.

"Keep this on it," he said. "It'll help with swelling."

Grace's eyelids drooped. Before she knew it, she felt herself being carried into Joy's bedroom and then laid down on the bed, a light kiss brushing against her forehead.

CHAPTER EIGHTEEN

"You're not doing this," Jaime told Grace three days later. "I told you to stay out of this."

He knew his tone was harsh, but seeing the bruise marring her cheek, he knew he had to be firm. Grace was as stubborn as they came, and she refused to back down.

"I've been working with Kat to hack into Eric's computer —" At Jaime's groan, she glared at him. "We're so close!"

"There is no 'we.' There is me, and that's it."

"So you're just going to throw whatever Kat's found to the wayside?"

He rubbed his temples. He didn't know what to do, except that he wanted to beat Eric within an inch of his life. The coward had retreated to his apartment and, as far as Jaime knew, hadn't left Heron's Landing. Probably still licking his wounds.

Despite his threats, Jaime knew very well that this thing wasn't over. It wouldn't be over until Eric was charged and Jaime was cleared of everything regarding the missing money from the vineyard.

After Eric had attacked Grace, he'd wanted to go the police, but Grace had been the one to stop him. "They'll just arrest you for assault," she'd pleaded. "They'll say you instigated it because that's what Eric will say. You aren't the one they'll want to believe."

He'd hated to admit that she'd been right. He'd expected Eric to call the police, but so far, nothing. He had no idea what the man's next move was, but he was going to do something before that happened.

He stood up from his kitchen table, where he and Grace had been sitting. He'd made her pancakes—at her request—and he picked up the plates to take them over to the sink. "I'll contact Kat myself," he said as he turned on the faucet. "Tell her you've had to stop being involved." He scrubbed at the plate. "I also don't want Kat getting hurt."

Grace put a hand on his arm. "She won't, because Eric won't find out. I told her beforehand the risks. She thought it was worth it. Because you are worth it, Jaime."

He couldn't help but grin. "Like the commercial? 'Because I'm worth it'?" He tossed his head like he was in a shampoo commercial.

Grace pinched him and he yelped. "Be serious."

He just looked at her.

"Okay, you are being serious. But so am I. I want to help, not sit on the sidelines like some useless damsel."

He shut off the water, turning to her. "You'll never be useless, but you were already hurt." He touched her bruised cheek, resolve filling him. "I can't let that happen again."

She just sighed.

Although Grace agreed that she wouldn't snoop around the vineyard anymore, she said that she would like to come with him to meet with Kat. Knowing this wasn't a battle he was going to win, he reluctantly agreed. The three of them would meet at Joy's later that evening, Joy also attending (considering it was her apartment).

"So what exactly are we doing tonight?" Joy asked as she, Grace and Jaime sat on her couch. The same couch they'd made love on only a few days prior. Jaime tried not to think about that too much, but his vision filled with Grace's hair down, her body trembling against his…

"Kat's showing us what she found," Grace replied. "She said she'd be here by eight o'clock."

"And this is supposed to prove Jaime is innocent?" Joy asked with an eyebrow raise.

"Supposedly. But I'm not sure how we'll manage that considering hacking into someone's email is considered illegal." Jaime gave Grace a look, which she patently ignored.

"Well, good thing I told Adam I was busy cleaning my bathroom tonight, otherwise he would've shown up, too, and wouldn't that have been great?" Joy made a face.

Grace had decided to lay low after Eric's assault, mostly so she wouldn't worry her family. Although her face was still bruised, it hadn't turned as bright purple as they were expecting, and soon she'd be able to cover it with makeup. Only Joy knew what had happened, and soon, Kat. Joy had wanted to go to the police immediately, but Grace had dissuaded her like she'd dissuaded Jaime.

A knock sounded on the door. Jaime got up to answer it. He'd never met Kat before although he'd seen her around town a handful of times. She eyed him when he opened the door, like some kind of science experiment. She wore glasses and red lipstick with her hair in tiny braids that were pulled into a bun on top of her head. She wore bright red skinny jeans underneath a puffy coat with heeled boots that clicked as she walked. Despite her small stature, she seemed to take up the room. After Jaime closed the door, she held out her hand.

"Kat Williamson. I'm assuming you're the guy we're all talking about?"

He took her hand; her grip was firm and sure. "Apparently. I'm Jaime."

"Great. Let me just get set up…" Kat walked into the living room, where she greeted Joy and Grace, asking Joy what her Wi-Fi password was. After she sat down, Jaime followed suit, sitting next to Grace on the couch.

"So, did Grace tell you what this was about?" Kat eyed them, pushing her glasses up her nose.

"Kind of. She just said that she talked to you about the investigation." Joy sipped her wine.

"Before we start, though, I just want to make sure you know that this could be dangerous for you." Jaime glanced at Grace, who wasn't looking at him. "I don't want to put you into any kind of position."

Kat looked at Grace, and although Jaime could tell that the bruise on Grace's cheek surprised her, she was subtle about it. Just a brow lift and nothing more.

"Grace let me know the risks from the beginning. Or rather, I figured them out for myself. But I'm not much for letting innocent people go to jail. Besides, Eric O'Neill is a scummy worm who grabbed my ass at the library, so I'm all about taking him down," Kat said.

Jaime couldn't help but smile. "Good to know. Let's get going then."

Kat had them stand behind her as she showed them what she'd found. She'd hacked into Eric's personal laptop fairly easily—he didn't exactly have high-tech security on his accounts—and utilizing a proxy IP address and other covert technology that made Jaime's brain spin, she showed them what she'd found.

"I must admit, this was easier than I expected," Kat explained, bringing up a series of emails. "I thought he wouldn't be stupid enough to leave a paper trail of what he planned to do. But I should've known that he's an idiot, too." She pointed to one of the emails, highlighting a paragraph. "Granted, he used an email without his name attached, but that was it. Didn't change his IP address, nothing. Here it says that he began to put his plan into motion."

Jaime's gaze roved the words before he narrowed his eyes. "This doesn't have anything specific enough to implicate him, though."

Kat shrugged. "No, but it's definitely shady. Here's another email. But really, here's the clincher. He'd been emailing with a vendor about raising prices. Now, that's a classic embezzlement move."

"It is?" Grace asked.

"Sure. Raise the price, the company pays, then you and the vendor split the difference."

Kat continued, showing them each and every bit of evidence she'd collected. By the end, Jaime was certain that no one could dismiss Eric's involvement. Especially when Kat showed them an email that specifically mentioned framing Jaime for all of it.

"This is all great," Jaime said as he sat back on the couch, "but we can't exactly take this to the police."

Kat smiled. "No, but you can use it. Nothing like a solid bluff to get a coward like Eric to shake in his cheap-ass boots."

They talked about what Kat had found for a while longer, until Kat realized what time it was, stating she had to get up early for work. Jaime had forgotten that she worked at the elementary school.

"I'll show you out," he said.

As they left Joy's apartment, a door opened at the end of the hall. Gavin, the prodigal Danvers brother, stepped out, looking like he'd been run over by a train.

Jaime hadn't met Gavin yet, but he'd recognize him anywhere. He had the Danvers look, and his eyes were the same as Grace's. He wondered if he should introduce himself, given the circumstances, but Gavin beat him to the punch.

"You must be Jaime," he said, extending his hand. "I'm Gavin Danvers."

Jaime shook his hand. "I heard you were back in Heron's Landing. How are you liking it?"

Gavin shrugged. "It's Heron's Landing. It is what it is." His gaze turned toward Kat, and Jaime could see his eyes widen ever so slightly.

Jaime glanced at the two of them. "Gavin, this is Kat Williamson."

They shook hands. Kat smiled as she did so, like she'd been told some wonderful secret. "You're Emma's dad, right? I have her in my computer class at HL Elementary."

"So you're the famous Ms. Williamson." To Jaime's surprise, the man actually smiled. It seemed a bit creaky, like he hadn't smiled in a long time. "Emma can't stop talking about you."

"I shouldn't say this, but she's definitely one of my favorite students."

Gavin seemed relieved, like he'd been expecting something else. "That's great to hear."

The two gazed at each other, and Jaime could feel the tension building between them. Kat licked her lips, and Gavin's gaze narrowed in on that small movement.

Suddenly flustered, Kat said in a rushed breath, "I need to get going. Jaime, Gavin, it was nice meeting you both." She nodded and then went down the stairs, not even pausing to let them say goodbye.

The two men stood at the top of the stairs, saying nothing. Gavin let out a breath.

Well, that was interesting, Jaime thought as he returned to Joy's apartment.

It LOOKED like snow when Jaime arrived at River's Bend. Gray clouds pushed in from the south, and the wind had a bite to it that clawed underneath the heaviest coats. It was only a few days before Christmas, and the vineyard sparkled with Christmas lights, more than one tree decorated and placed in front of the tall windows.

But Jaime wasn't here to look at Christmas lights. He'd called Eric yesterday to ask to meet with him. He could've gone to his place, he supposed, but he wanted to speak to him on somewhat neutral territory.

He glanced up at the sky, squinting at what looked like tiny flurries. He hoped it wouldn't start snowing before this was over and done with.

A car pulled up. Jaime stilled, listening as he stood behind the main building of the vineyard, waiting for Eric to arrive. His former sous chef looked like hell as he walked toward him, his face a motley of bruises. Jaime rather wished he'd broken the man's arm and maybe some toes, but seeing Eric clutch at his ribs as he walked gave him some satisfaction at least.

They stared at each other. Jaime rather felt like this was some kind of gun battle, with the swirling wind and the silence hanging between them. He'd laugh if he weren't so tired, so angry with everything.

"I'm assuming you didn't want to meet just to stand outside and freeze our asses off?" Eric stuffed his hands into the pockets of his coat, scowling above his scarf.

"Let's not waste each other's time, shall we?" Jaime stepped toward Eric, keeping eye contact the entire time. "The jig is up, Eric. We all know you're the one who's been stealing from River's Bend and setting me up to take the fall."

Eric laughed, a scratchy laugh that made Jaime want to throttle him. "And what evidence do you have? That's right, none. Just because you want it to be true doesn't mean one fucking thing."

Jaime pulled out a sheaf of papers. This was the tricky part. Although they did have evidence, it wasn't evidence they had gotten legally. So he had to bluff his way through this, and hope that Eric wouldn't call his bluff.

"We have financial statements from the vineyard, copies of invoices, and even a statement from the vendor who you were working with." The last was a lie, but Eric didn't know that.

The younger man's scowl remained. "I don't believe you."

Jaime shrugged. "Does it matter? We have evidence that implicates you and clears me."

"You've already been charged with the crime."

"Based on flimsy evidence." Jaime slapped at the papers. "This is concrete, my friend. This shows that you're a weaselly piece of shit who would do anything to screw me over for God only knows why."

Eric's eyes darted around. "You really have no idea, do you?"

"About what?"

"I'm not the piece of shit," he growled, his face turning red. "I'm not the one charged with a crime, and then had the audacity to start fucking your boss's sister. But now you've turned Grace into your little whore—"

Jaime grabbed him by the collar and pushed him against the wall before Eric realized what was happening. "Do not *ever* speak of Grace that way," Jaime hissed, his vision turning red. "I already warned you once. Do you want me to break every rib, every finger, every toe, every bone in your body? Because if you even so much as think of Grace, I'll make you pay."

Eric gasped for breath. Jaime let him go, and Eric rubbed his throat, swearing.

"I want to get this over with. I have the evidence that will send you to jail, and even if some jury finds you innocent, we all know that the scandal will destroy you and your family." Jaime watched as Eric's eyes widened, the first bit of fear crossing his face. "Ah, so now you care? Eric O'Neill, the son of the prominent senator, getting arrested for embezzlement. That'll make his campaign a hard sell, don't you think?"

Eric spat. "Fuck you, Martínez."

"You're the one who's fucked. Either I take this evidence to the police, or you disappear from my sight. Either way, once your father finds out, I'm sure you won't get a cent of his money."

Eric's face got progressively redder, his eyes flashing. Jaime stood and waited for him to give in. The O'Neills were such a prominent family in the state and country that any hint of scandal like this would be a huge coup. Jaime hadn't known how much Eric would care about something like that, but clearly, it mattered.

"So what's it gonna be, Eric?"

Eric refused to look at him. He stared at the ground, like it would give him some kind of an answer to Jaime's question. Jaime could feel the wind picking up, and snowflakes melted against his face as the clouds opened up.

"Either give me an answer or I'm taking this to the police." When Eric didn't reply, Jaime began counting down. "Five… four…three…two…"

Eric stood up and, reaching into his coat pocket, pulled out a gun. His arms trembled as he held it, but Jaime stilled as he aimed it straight at his head. The snow began falling faster around them.

"Fuck you. Fuck you and everything you stand for," Eric said. "You can't make me do anything. You're going to jail because you're the one they want, not me."

An odd sense of calm enveloped Jaime. Perhaps he knew that Eric didn't have the balls to shoot him. Or maybe this was just how you felt before your last moments. If he was supposed to die here today, he only hoped that Grace would find happiness.

But Jaime didn't want to die here today in cold blood. He

held up his hands, placating Eric. "You don't want to do this," he said in a low voice.

The gun trembled in Eric's hands. "Yes, I do. I've dreamed about shooting your brains out. It would be worth it." But his voice bespoke his fear, and his eyes were wild.

Jaime stepped toward him slowly. "Put the gun down, Eric."

"Fuck you. Stay away from me!"

Jaime stopped. His heart hammered so hard he could barely breathe. Snow fell on his face, melting against his hot skin.

And then before he could say another word: a gunshot, deafening the world around him.

CHAPTER NINETEEN

G race sat at Joy's and stared at the clock. The minute hand seemed to slow down with each passing second, until she had to stand up and pace around the room. Joy watched her, saying nothing, because there really wasn't anything that could be said.

Jaime was out there confronting Eric because he was a brave idiot and she hated him as much as she adored him. She wanted to be there for him, but he'd made her promise she'd stay put. So she had. She waited, and she paced, and she prayed that this would be over before the sun lowered below the horizon that day.

"Grace, you're giving me a headache. Come sit down at least." Joy patted the couch cushion next to her.

"I can't. I can't sit still." Grace wrung her hands. She felt like an army wife left behind while her husband was deployed. Except her man was only a few miles away, and with every passing minute, she wondered why she'd agreed not to go with him.

A knock sounded on the door. Joy raised an eyebrow and

then after looking through the peephole, opened the door to allow both Adam and Gavin inside.

Grace turned. When her brothers saw her, their eyes widened.

"Grace, what the hell happened to you?" Adam demanded as he came toward her.

"Was it that boyfriend of yours?" Gavin gritted his teeth. "I swear to God, I'll kill him myself…"

Grace put up her hands to stem the tide of male rage. "No, no, Jaime would never hurt me." She touched her cheek. She'd thought she'd put enough makeup on to cover it, but apparently not.

Gavin tilted her face so he could inspect the bruise closer. "Who did this?" His voice was low, dangerous. Grace had to stop herself from shivering. While Adam was a bundle of rage, Gavin's anger was quieter.

"Eric O'Neill attacked me. Jaime is with him right now."

Both men yelled, "What!" at the same time, and then the questions started pouring in. Joy, seeing that Grace was about to tell them to go away, tugged the Danvers brothers to the couch, made them sit, and told all three of them that they were going to discuss this *like adults* and not do anything *stupid*.

"He hit my little sister! Are you pressing charges? Why didn't you go to the police?" Adam was about to stand up, but Joy pushed him back down onto the couch.

"Let your sister talk," Joy said, pointing a finger in his face. "Yelling over her isn't going to help."

"I'm not yelling!" he yelled.

Grace just buried her face in her hands.

After Joy had gotten the two brothers to quiet somewhat,

Grace told the story as best she could. Adam looked close to storming out to enact some kind of medieval vengeance, while Gavin listened more attentively, but with an equal amount of rage. Joy sat next to her fiancé, and he held her hand, like her physical presence barely tethered him.

"So he's with him right now?" Gavin leaned forward. "Why does he expect to do? Have some kind of duel?"

"He wants this over and done with. I told him it would be dangerous, but he's stubborn." Grace felt tears press at her eyelids. "I'm so afraid for him. Eric is a loose cannon…"

As she spoke, Adam turned pale. Joy noticed and pulled at his arm. "Hey, what is that face?" she asked. "You're scaring me."

"As I was driving here, I heard gun shots." Adam licked his lips; his eyes were stark. "I thought it was deer hunters, but now…"

Grace didn't stay to listen to anything else. She grabbed her phone, stuffed her feet into her boots, and threw her coat on as the sound of her brothers' shouts followed her. She didn't hear anything as she got into her car and began driving the few miles to River's Bend. She barely heard the operator at the end of her call to 911, and she didn't recognize her own voice: strangely calm and level. She gripped the steering wheel until her knuckles turned white.

When she got to the vineyard in record time, she hid her car some distance away and began running. She heard shouts as she neared the main building, and then there was another gunshot. She covered her mouth to stifle a scream.

Running, she went to the back of the building, hiding herself in an alcove. She knew Jaime would kill her if he saw her, but she couldn't simply just stand around and let him die.

She gazed around the corner and saw that both men were still standing. No one was bleeding, as far as she could tell. Jaime was trying to get Eric to calm down as he continued to wave his gun, his expression frantic.

"Don't do this," Jaime said. "You don't have to do this."

"You've given me no choice!" Eric leveled the gun at Jaime once more.

Grace wondered if the earlier shots were warning shots. Or perhaps Eric's aim had been too abysmal to hit his target, given his emotional state. She watched, horrified, as a gun was pointed at the man she loved, and she knew there was nothing she could do to stop it.

Then, the blessed sound of sirens. Eric wheeled around, and a group of cops converged on him.

"Drop your weapon!" When Eric didn't move, the officer shouted once again, "Drop your weapon!"

Eric bent down and placed his gun on the ground. Before Grace could even blink, he was surrounded and on the ground, his arms behind his back as he was handcuffed.

Grace saw Jaime take a deep breath, leaning over to put his hands on his thighs. She didn't think. She just ran out and wrapped him in a huge hug, burying her face in his shoulder.

"Grace...*Grace*, what are you doing here?" He hugged her back, so hard her ribs ached. "What the hell are you doing here?"

He tilted her face up so he could look at her.

"Adam heard gunshots and I didn't think, I just knew I couldn't let you do this. You could've died." She covered her mouth to keep the sobs from pouring from her throat.

"Jesus Christ, you fool." Jaime kissed her, then kissed her

cheeks, her nose, her chin. "You stupid little fool. God, Graciela, I told you to stay put!"

"And I told you this was too dangerous for you to do alone!"

After that, no more words were needed. They couldn't stop touching each other, couldn't stop kissing, like if they broke physical contact, one would disappear into the ether. Jaime could call her a fool over and over again, but she didn't have the strength to get angry about it. They were both fools.

Everything moved quickly. Eric was taken away, and the remaining officers interviewed Jaime and Grace. One of the officers was none other than Sheriff Jennings, who gave them both a look like he wasn't remotely surprised they were involved in something like this. Coming up to them, his hands at his belt, he scowled at the two of them.

"Can you tell me what happened here?"

Grace glanced at Jaime. He cleared his throat, and then replied in a level voice, "I'd prefer to get in contact with my lawyer before making any statements."

The sheriff merely harrumphed, but nodded. Before he turned away, though, he said, "You've gotten into quite a number of binds around here, Mr. Martínez. One wonders how much longer you can stay in Heron's Landing without burning the whole place down."

Grace held onto Jaime's arm, feeling him tense from the insult. Medics came to attend to them, which they both waved off. Grace just wanted to go home. After some more questions and then even more questions from Adam, Gavin and Joy, who had shown up soon after, Grace and Jaime headed back to his place.

"You'll be all right?" Joy asked her. "You don't want to

come back to my place?"

Grace shook her head. "I'll be all right. I'll text you later."

Grace's phone started exploding with phone calls from her parents and pretty much everyone else in the town. No one could believe what had happened, and rumors swirled ravenously. One story said that Jaime had tried to shoot Eric in the head, while another said that Eric was a part of the mob and had been hired to take Jaime out on some hit job.

Grace talked briefly with her mother, assuring her she was all right.

"Come home as soon as you can," Julia said, her voice wavering. "We miss you. We were so scared for you, honey. I know you and your father aren't agreeing lately, but we both love you so much."

Tears sprang to Grace's eyes. "I know. I love you guys too. I'll talk to you later."

Jaime muttered something about eating. Grace wasn't hungry, but he seemed to need to cook something. She heard him puttering about the kitchen, swearing and chopping and sautéing what seemed like everything in his fridge. She sat on the couch and tried to wrap her head around everything that had happened.

Her brain wouldn't work, though. She kept remembering the sound of those gunshots, the way Eric had pointed that gun at Jaime. She closed her eyes and it was all she could see.

"Don't think about it," Jaime said as he sat a plate in front of her. "You'll drive yourself crazy."

She stared at the grilled cheese in front of her, and her stomach turned. "I can't eat anything."

"At least drink something."

She forced herself to swallow some water, which helped

her feel a little bit better. But she just leaned her head against Jaime's shoulder as he ate.

"My parents were in El Salvador right as the civil war began," he said softly, not looking at her. "They've never told me everything they saw, but I know that some of their best friends and so many family members just…disappeared. When I asked them how they coped, they said all they could do at the time was look forward. If you look back, the past will take over your future."

Grace rubbed his back. "I'm so glad you're all right. The thought of you out there, that gun…" She choked back a sob.

He turned toward her, pulling her into his arms. "Don't think about it. Don't. It's over. It's over, Graciela. Even if they still charge me, Eric won't be getting out any time soon for attempted murder. You're safe, I'm safe."

She shook her head. "You're not safe if you end up going to jail, too!" She plucked at his shirt, like she could find the answers she was looking for in the weave of the cotton. "I want to help you. I want to, but how can I? You shouldn't have to do this alone."

Jaime just held her. They held each other as afternoon turned into evening.

Grace's phone rang. Seeing that it was her mother again, she said, "I should probably go home."

He nodded. "They're worried about you."

"Will you be all right by yourself?"

"Go, Graciela. I'll see you tomorrow."

She leaned down to kiss him, and he hauled her into his lap, kissing her until she gasped for air. He murmured her name against her hair.

"I have to go," she said, extricating herself from his arms.

He kissed her fingers before he finally let go.

GRACE COULD BARELY COMPREHEND the passing of time anymore. She didn't see Jaime again until three days later, despite calling him multiple times. He'd told her he was busy talking to his newly hired lawyer, to the cops, and everything was such a mess that he hadn't had time to come by to see her.

Although she missed him, she was glad to get home for a bit. Julia hovered over her, especially once she saw the bruise on her cheek, and Grace had cried in her arms for a while, a cleansing kind of cry that made her feel somewhat better. Carl—never particularly demonstrative—embraced Grace in a bone-crushing hug, and although there was still anger and frustration between them, she realized that her father loved her, in his own way. She'd hugged him back, hoping that they could return to what their relationship had once been.

On Monday, Christmas Day arrived. Grace had forgotten about it in the swirl of events, although the Danvers house was suitably decorated with the requisite tree, lights, and various Santa figurines. That morning, Grace came downstairs to find her entire family—including both brothers, Joy, and Emma—all in the living room. They exchanged presents and ate a Christmas breakfast. Grace had neglected to buy anyone a present, for which she apologized profusely. Julia had merely leaned over and rubbed her arm, telling her she didn't need to worry about that.

The rest of the day was spent playing with Emma's new toys—Grace sat on the floor with her niece next to her as they dressed dolls and built Lego sets—and although she couldn't stop thinking about Jaime and wished he could be here, she also was glad to be with her family now. She'd missed them. They drove her crazy most days, but they were still her family.

But when it began snowing later that evening, Grace stood at the window and felt tears fall. She didn't know. She just knew something was going to happen.

Emma came up to her. Her blue eyes gazed up at her. She didn't say a thing, but just leaned against Grace, holding her hand. Grace placed a hand on her hair, stroking her blonde locks, and she let the tears fall just as the snow outside fell across the land.

Jaime called her to say that they needed to talk. The following morning, she met him at his house, the snow still falling. She stamped her boots and brushed off the snow from her coat as she came inside, shivering.

He came up and took her coat before handing her a mug of hot cider. "Freshly made," he said.

She inhaled the scent of cinnamon and apples and sighed.

Once sitting, she drank her cider and waited, knowing that Jaime needed to get whatever it was he needed to get out —out.. As the silence lengthened, anxiety started filling her. She remembered her tears from last night, and it had seemed like a premonition of some sort.

She sat her mug down on the coffee table.

"I'm leaving," he said, not looking at her.

The words didn't register. "Leaving…?"

"Leaving Heron's Landing."

She stared at him, her eyes widening. She wasn't surprised, and yet, hearing the words was another thing entirely. "For how long?" she whispered.

He finally caught her gaze. His face was sad, resigned, but also stubborn. "For good."

"But what about your job? The vineyard?" *What about me?*

"I don't have a job anymore. Do you think Adam wants to keep me on?" Jaime ran his fingers through his hair. "No, I can't stay here. I can't stay in a place that thought I was capable of stealing from my friend."

Her lower lip quivered, but she bit it to stem the tide of tears. She was tired of crying, tired of feeling like her heart was breaking. "So that's it? It's just over?"

Getting up, he kneeled in front of her, taking her hands. "We both knew this was temporary," he said softly. "It could never have worked, Graciela. Not with everything that's happened."

"What does that even mean?" She yanked her hands away. "I was just some kind of fling for you?"

He shook his head. "No, but you're young...you don't know what you want."

She laughed an incredulous laugh. "Because you know exactly what I want? You have a lot of gall. I'm not some little kid, Jaime."

"I never said you were."

"Does it matter to you that I'm in love with you?" As his face crumpled, she added, "There's nothing for you here? *I'm* here."

He took her hands again. "Graciela, I care about you. Deeply. But I can't stay. I know you understand this. And as far as being in love with me... You'll move on. You told me yourself you had a crush on me. What's to say this isn't just a crush, too?"

She couldn't speak. She just stared at him, confused and angry and heartbroken.

"You're just going to run away then. You're going to abandon everything you've built here because of one man. Isn't this what Eric would've wanted? For you to be run out of town like some criminal?"

Jaime didn't say anything, but he wouldn't look at her, either.

Standing up, she began putting her boots back on. But her hands were shaking so much she couldn't get them over her heel, and she swore.

Jaime got up and steadied her. "Grace, I'm sorry," he whispered.

She whirled on him. "You're sorry? You're sorry that you just threw my love for you back in my face?" She got her coat, holding it up in front of her like a shield. "Maybe it was a crush in the beginning, when I first met you. When you walked me home in the rain underneath your umbrella, and you got wet while I stayed dry." She looked at him, and all she could see was his clenched jaw and his vacant eyes. "Do you remember that?"

He looked away. "I'm sorry, I don't."

She opened the door, not even bothering to put on her coat, a sob breaking forth. He grabbed her arm and said in a low voice, "I'm sorry, Grace. Just know that I'm sorry."

Yanking her arm away, she opened the door and raced out into the snow, her heart cut to ribbons. She drove home and collapsed on her bed, where she cried until she couldn't cry one more tear.

It's over, was the only thought in her head. *It's over, and I'll probably never see him again.*

CHAPTER TWENTY

December changed into January and then February, and Jaime had been gone from Heron's Landing for two months. Two long months, where he'd stayed in St. Louis with his parents to figure out what the hell he was going to do with his life.

He'd shown up at his parents' place a few days before New Year's. His mother had looked at him for just a second before she ushered him inside and plied him with more food than any one person could eat, while his father stood over them, his face creased in concern. Jaime had told them the entire story—they'd already known about Eric getting arrested—and he'd mentioned Grace more than once. His parents had looked at each other, but said nothing.

His father Fernando sat next to him on the floral couch Jaime's mother had bought over twenty years ago, and said in Spanish, "You can stay with us as long as you need, Jaimito."

If he hadn't been so exhausted, he would've cried in relief.

The charges were still very much in the back of his mind, though. After hiring the best lawyer he could afford, Jaime had tried to live his life as normally as possible while he let the officials do their work. His lawyer was gathering evidence while also using Eric's attempted murder as an obvious piece of the puzzle. No man who doesn't have something to hide would do something like that, his lawyer argued. The police—headed by Sheriff Jennings—weren't quite as interested in admitting they'd been wrong, and thus, things were moving slowly and without much progress that Jaime could see.

Jaime had begun applying for jobs all over the country as an executive chef. From San Francisco to New York City to Miami, he'd sent in applications and resumes and CVs and cover letters and although he'd gotten a few bites, at the moment, he still had no firm offer. He could only hope that changed, as he hated living off of his parents' charity any longer than necessary.

Of course, all of this was a mere distraction from what truly kept him awake at night: Grace. Grace, and the way she'd looked at him when he'd said she wasn't really in love with him but that it was just a crush. With how she asked him about walking with her in the rain, and his response. *I don't remember*, he'd said.

He'd lied about that, too.

He remembered young Grace, getting caught in the rain. He remembered rushing to her with his umbrella, and he remembered how she had barely said a word to him as he'd walked her home. He remembered how the rain soaked his shirt to his skin, but his umbrella had kept her dry the entire way. When he'd dropped her off at her house, she'd looked at him like he was her knight in shining armor, and it had unmanned him. So he'd ignored it because that was easier.

He hadn't heard from Grace since he'd told her was

leaving Heron's Landing. That hadn't surprised him. He missed her, though, with an ache that he was certain would never leave him. He missed her smile, and her laugh, and the way her long hair fell about them like a curtain when they made love, and he missed how she'd looked at him like he was a miracle she couldn't believe she'd discovered.

It was mid-February. The days were still cold and it had snowed just last week. Sitting at his parents' kitchen table, Jaime heard the front door open. Fernando walked in, briefcase in hand. His father was in the middle of midterms already, and was often on campus seeing desperate undergraduates and sleep-deprived grad students in his office. Fernando got a cup of coffee that Jaime had made hours earlier and sat across from him at the pockmarked table.

The two men sat in companionable silence. This was one thing Jaime had always appreciated about his father: he never forced conversation when it wasn't needed.

But today, Fernando seemed in the mood to talk.

"Any leads today?" he asked in Spanish. They always spoke in Spanish amongst each other, and it always reminded Jaime of home.

"Nothing today. But I have a phone interview on Friday."

"Excellent. You'll have a new job before you know it, and then you'll get out of this place for good." Fernando pushed his wired glasses up his nose. "I never thought you'd stay in that little town for long, Jaimito. Too cloying, too small, for one such as you."

Jaime smiled. "I never thought I'd be there that long, either."

"Then again, sometimes we end up in places we'd never expect. I never thought I'd move to the States with your mother. Yet here we are. As a young man, I never wanted to leave San Salvador. Why should I? But sometimes life turns out differently."

Jaime gazed at his father. "Do you miss El Salvador?"

Fernando let out a breath. "Sometimes. I miss hearing Spanish like that every day. I miss the food, the smells. I hate snow." He smiled wryly. "But this is our home now, even though there are days I'd like to go back."

Jaime knew a huge reason why his parents had never returned was because of the civil war that had destroyed the country. They'd watched from afar as the country they loved, that they'd grown up in, was filled with violence and bloodshed. He couldn't imagine how it must have felt, not knowing what would happen to friends and family left behind.

It put things in perspective, he supposed. He'd been to hell and back again these past few months, but he'd survived. He'd move on. And he'd live his life and be as happy as he could manage.

"Just don't punish yourself for things out of your control," Fernando said quietly. "Grasp happiness with both hands if it's offered to you. Even if it's in a town you never thought you'd come to care about."

Jaime couldn't say anything. He just nodded, and hoped his father didn't notice how he wiped his eyes on his sleeve.

It was late at night, when the only sound he could hear was the creaking of his parents' old house, that he realized that he loved Grace. He loved her so much it took his breath away. He murmured the words into the darkness, and it was almost like she was there with him. But when he opened his eyes, he was alone, and his heart sank as he thought that it was probably too late to tell her how he felt.

On Friday morning, Jaime had his phone interview for a position in New York City, which he thought went well. The head of human resources told him they'd contact him shortly to let him know if they would move forward with an in-person interview. All of that faded into the background, though, when he got a call from his lawyer David Wilson.

"Jaime, good news," Wilson said. He was a younger man, but so full of drive and enthusiasm that when he'd heard about Jaime's case, he'd taken it on immediately. "I just got a call from the DA, and the charges against you have been dropped. We did it."

"Are you serious?"

"Completely. It's over. You're a free man. They've all been dismissed, and Eric O'Neill is now being charged with both embezzlement and attempted murder. He's currently being held in a psych ward, since they believe he could be a danger to himself and to others."

Jaime only shook his head, incredulous. "I can't believe this."

"Believe it." Wilson seemed to be shuffling through papers as he spoke on the phone. "I have a meeting here in the next minute, but I also wanted to let you know that a big reason they were dropped was because—oh what's her name, here it is—Grace Danvers? Do you know her? Well, she apparently wouldn't let this go. She put together enough evidence that the DA couldn't ignore it. Interesting, right?"

Jaime had to sit down. "Yeah, interesting," he whispered.

"Hey, I have to go. I'll talk to you soon."

Staring at his phone, Jaime didn't know what to feel. Relief, incredulity. Shock. Love. Grace had done this. He didn't know how or why, but she'd done this. She hadn't given up on him, when he'd given up on her. Burying his face in his hands, he groaned. God, what had he done?

He called the one person he knew would have answers.

"This is Adam."

"Adam, what did she do?" Jaime asked, not bothering with saying hello.

Adam sighed. "She worked with Kat, as far as I know. She was pretty secretive about the whole thing, although I do know she was close to landing in hot water because of it." His tone turned stern. "She put her neck on the line for you. And quite frankly, I'm not sure you deserved it."

"I didn't. Your sister—no one deserves her." Jaime ran his fingers through his hair. "My God."

"Yeah, that was pretty much my reaction." Adam paused. "I don't understand what happened, but you've been missed. Not just by Grace. Me, Joy. Everyone. I know you probably don't want to return, but there's always a place for you at River's Bend. I haven't even begun to replace you."

Warmth filled Jaime's chest. "Thank you. I'll talk to you later, okay?"

"Just don't do anything stupid," Adam said wryly before they both said goodbye.

Jaime began packing his things, his mind whirling. He had to get back to Heron's Landing. He had to tell Grace he loved her—he adored her, he couldn't live without her. He didn't even know what he was packing and he was probably leaving behind half of his stuff, but he had to get out of here. But then logic rammed into his euphoria, and he knew he couldn't run back to Heron's Landing just yet.

His parents' citizenship interview was the following Monday, and Jaime had agreed to be with them when they went. Despite the charges and subsequent arrest, Immigration had allowed his parents to continue with their application, for which Jaime was infinitely grateful.

He unpacked his things, forcing himself to think. Just because Grace had worked to get his charges dropped didn't mean she'd take him back. He'd hurt her. He wracked his brain to figure out what he could do to show her how much he cared, but beyond groveling at her feet, he was at a loss.

He told his parents about the charges being dropped that night, although he didn't tell them about Grace's involvement. Ana had cried and both of his parents had hugged him close, thanking God for his mercy.

Fernando and Ana got ready for their interviews that Monday morning, with Jaime helping to straighten his father's tie and assuring his mother that she looked beautiful. The rest of the day was taken up with waiting, interviewing, and more waiting, and although Jaime couldn't assure his parents that their interviews had been successful, he could only hope that things went well for them. He knew how much stress this entire process had placed on them, besides the enormous expense.

Afterward, he told Fernando about Grace's involvement in getting the charges dropped. His father's eyes had widened, and he didn't say anything for a while. It was only after Jaime had asked him his thoughts that Fernando asked, "What are you doing, still sitting here, Jaimito? Go tell the girl you love her!"

It was Wednesday afternoon when Jaime drove into Heron's Landing, almost exactly two months since he'd left. While driving there, he got a call from the restaurant in New York City.

"We want to offer you the position," the woman at the other end said. "No further interviewing is necessary. Your resume and your experience is enough for us to make a decision. We'd like you to start right away, if possible."

Jaime could barely comprehend the woman's words. He'd wanted a position like this for so long, a job in a big city instead of the middle of nowhere, but now he hesitated. Is this what he really wanted?

"May I think about it?" he asked finally.

The woman made assuring noises. "Of course. Give me a call whenever you'd like to discuss salary and whatnot. But please know we want to move quickly on this."

Jaime hung up just as it began pouring rain, and it rained all the way to Heron's Landing. Driving onto the unpaved road that led to Grace's house, Jaime felt his car lurch. When he pressed the gas, his car squealed but didn't move. He swore. Getting out, he realized he was stuck in the mud. Rain pounded down around him, soaking him instantly; he went back inside his car to call a tow truck, but he swore again when he saw that he had no service.

He got out of the car, putting his jacket over his head as a makeshift umbrella. He'd just have to walk to the Danvers' place. But as he shut his car door, he saw something out in the distance. A figure stood in the rain, and as he walked toward it, he realized with a start that it was Grace.

CHAPTER TWENTY-ONE

After her shift at Trudy's, Grace had hoped to get home before the rain started. But as was her luck, it started right when she was halfway between Trudy's and her house, and to make it even worse, it poured buckets. It was that cold kind of winter rain that soaked into your very bones, but it was so muddy that she couldn't move faster than a quick walk. She was just thankful Trudy had let her borrow her giant black umbrella.

As she walked along the road to her house, the rain continued to pound, although the trees provided a little bit of cover. Turning the bend, she saw a truck in the middle of the road, and her heart started pounding. She stood and stared, the rain falling around her, and she watched as Jaime walked around to the back of the truck. She couldn't move. She could only try to steady her breathing, but it was no use.

When he saw her, though? She didn't know if her vision blurred because of the rain or because of the tears spilling from her eyes.

"Grace!" He jogged toward her, and she met him, grabbing

onto his arm to keep from slipping in the mud. "Grace, what are you doing here?" he shouted over the rain.

She laughed. He was soaked to the skin and looked cold and miserable but she couldn't help laughing. "I should be asking you that!" She moved so the umbrella covered them both, and the rain beat down on top of them.

His face split into a wide smile. He covered her fingers that held the umbrella.

"Did you really do it? Work to get the charges dropped?" He gaze scanned her face, as if he could figure out the answer before she opened her mouth.

She faltered. Was that the only reason he came back? To thank her? Her heart clenched, and she looked away.

"When my lawyer told me...and then Adam..." Jaime reached out and touched her cheek. "Grace, why did you do it?"

Tears fell down her cheeks. "Do you really not know?" She gripped the umbrella tighter, her breath puffing. "You were right, though, about one thing. Before, it was a crush. You were a dream I created; it wasn't love that I felt for you."

He didn't say anything, but he just stared at her, his fingers clutching at her hand.

"But I realized that as I really got to know you—the real you, not the dream I'd created—that I fell in love with you. With *you*, Jaime. I love you. I know you don't feel the same, but I can't keep this to myself anymore—"

Before she could finish her sentence, he pulled her into his arms, umbrella still over them, and kissed her so hard that her breath left her body. He kissed her like he'd wanted to kiss her for years and years. He kissed her like she was the most precious person in the universe.

He kissed her like he loved her.

"Graciela, my God, you shatter me. I told you that before, didn't I? But it's true." He cupped her face in his hands, and the umbrella trembled over them. "I love you," he said, his voice low but sure and true. "I love you so much."

She made some kind of a noise—between a moan and a squeak and maybe a sob—and then she threw her arms around him, the umbrella falling into mud, kissing him for all she was worth. He laughed, pulling her close. The rain fell around them, soaking them, but it didn't matter. Nothing mattered except that they'd found each other.

"I got a job offer, in New York City." He brushed her hair off her forehead. "But I'm not going to take it. I want to stay here—with you."

"But I know you've dreamed of a position like that. Are you sure?"

He nodded. "I always thought I just wanted to get away from Heron's Landing. That it was just a pit stop. But then I met you, and my dream—it changed. Because *you* are my new dream."

Grace couldn't say anything, so she yanked on his jacket collar and pressed her mouth against his, and although his cheeks and nose were cold, his mouth was hot. She moaned against his lips. He tasted like peppermint and Jaime and everything she'd ever wanted. Pressing her hands against his chest, she felt his heart pound beneath her fingertips.

"Come on, let's get in the truck before we freeze to death," he said. He helped her inside, and then they were kissing and touching, making the windows of the truck steam. Jaime stripped out of his jacket while Grace peeled off hers, and it was only when he stopped to gaze into her eyes that he said, "You cut your hair."

Grace smiled. She'd cut her hair so it was a chin-length bob, and it had been freeing. A new beginning, especially when she'd thought she'd never see Jaime again. Now, he fingered the shortened locks, looking like he had no idea what to say. She hoped he liked it, and when he didn't say anything, she became self-conscious.

"I know it's short," she began, "but I thought I needed something new."

He ran his fingers through her hair, touching her chin as he did so. "I like it." Then he caught her gaze. "But you could be as bald as an egg and I'd love it, because it's *you.*"

She touched his hair, which was rather shaggy at the moment. "I'm not sure I could love you as well if you went bald," she teased. "I rather like your hair, you know."

He hauled her into his lap. "So you just like me for my looks? I never knew you were so shallow."

"There are so many things you don't know about me." She touched his mouth with a finger, which he kissed.

Looking outside at the falling rain, she laughed suddenly.

"What is it?" he asked.

"You said you didn't remember, but this is just like when you walked me home." She smiled at him, her eyes shining. "That was the day I fell in love with you, the first time, you know."

He brushed her cheek with his fingers. "I lied, you know, about not remembering." Her eyes widened slightly. "I remember seeing you that day, getting drenched, and how you wouldn't talk to me for the entire walk home."

"I was just too shy to talk to you. You held the umbrella over me while you got soaked."

He wrapped his arms around her waist again with her perched on his lap. "And I'd do it again. I love you, Graciela."

She laid her head against his chest, listening to his heartbeat as the rain fell outside their safe haven.

EPILOGUE

With the coming of spring came the beginning of wedding season once again. After hosting its sixth wedding, River's Bend started to come back to life. The harvest looked good, and with the revenue from weddings and other events, the vineyard began to turn a figurative new leaf. Soon, they'd actually be making money again.

Jaime had returned to his position as the executive chef, while Grace had decided to apply to grad school come the fall. After much debate with her parents, she moved in with Jaime after spring break, although Carl had not been particularly fond of his unmarried daughter "shacking up with his former employee." She'd also begun painting again, and although she was often frustrated with the results, Jaime had encouraged her to continue. One night, Grace had gotten up the courage to ask if him if he'd let her paint *him*—and in the nude, no less. Some painting had occurred, but things had devolved when Jaime started literally painting Grace before they toppled to the floor, laughing and kissing.

Now the trees were changing, and the white buds flourished on the pear trees. Going outside was like a petal tornado if the wind were blowing, and Grace loved every minute of it. When Jaime wasn't busy working, they would take walks around the town, and they particularly liked to go to the spot down by the river where they'd talked so many months ago.

Standing outside River's Bend at the beginning of May, Grace looked up at the clear sky, closing her eyes. It was the first really warm day of spring, and everyone it seemed had come to River's Bend's first annual farm to table event. Hosting chefs, farmers, and other merchants from across the state, the event bustled with activity. Grace had only seen Jaime this morning for a few moments before he'd had to go into work. Right now, he was giving a demonstration while his audience applauded.

"Having a good time?" Gavin walked up to her with Emma in tow. Emma clutched her dad's hand, as she was shy around crowds like this.

"I am. What about you? I feel like I haven't seen you two in ages." Grace smiled at her niece, who gave her a tentative smile back.

"Busy. My job wants me to return to Boston. They were never fond of me telecommuting, and now they think it'll be better in the long run if I return." Gavin grimaced. "But Emma just started school here, and I'd hate to make her start elsewhere a second time."

Emma didn't say anything. Grace was once again struck by how much her niece looked like her sister-in-law Teagan, but she also had the blonde hair that was common in the Danvers family.

"How is Teagan?" Grace asked softly.

"I haven't heard from her, but as far as I know, she's doing all right." He didn't volunteer any more information than that, and Grace couldn't blame him. She knew their divorce was soon to be finalized, and her mother had told her Gavin had signed and returned the divorce papers already.

Suddenly feeling awkward, Grace was relieved to see Kat walking up to them. She waved. "Kat!"

Kat smiled, returning the wave. Today she wore a blue dress with boots, her lipstick a shade of fuchsia that only she could pull off.

But Grace's attention was snagged when she saw Gavin stiffen as Kat approached. Kat didn't look at him, either, but instead focused her attention on Emma.

"Hey Emma," she said, "how's your spring break going?"

Emma shifted on her feet. "Okay," she murmured at her feet.

"You want to go get some funnel cake with me? I know I can't eat an entire one myself."

Emma nodded. Gavin seemed intent on not looking at Kat, which Grace found rather amusing.

Seeing that Jaime had finished his presentation, Grace said to no one in particular, "I'll let you guys go get that funnel cake."

"Bye, Grace," Kat said as Grace walked away.

Jaime was cleaning up his station, but when she approached, he stopped and embraced her. He kissed her lightly, and she smiled.

"What was that for?" She looked up at him.

"Because I wanted to. Besides, you look so pretty today. And if I'm lucky, maybe we'll get some time alone so I can show just how pretty I think you are."

She blushed and laughed. "You're ridiculous." But instead

of pulling away, she twined her arms around his neck and murmured, "Do you think you have time right now?"

His eyes gleamed. Before she could protest, he picked her up as she shrieked with laughter, taking her away to show her exactly what he'd meant.

~

KAT KNEW about a lot of things: she knew computers, she knew video games, she knew French, she knew how to fix a flat tire. She knew her Periodic Table, she knew how to diagram a sentence. She collected information like a bird, using it to build her mental nest, although the nest was never finished. You could never stop learning, never stop discovering.

But as she stood next to Gavin Danvers—grim, taciturn, tall, dark and handsome Gavin Danvers—she had no wealth of knowledge to understand why he affected her so much. He wasn't even touching her, but simply having him stand next to her was enough to put her on alert, like an electrical buzzing through her veins. She gripped her bag tighter, like it could keep her from disintegrating into a pile of mush at his feet.

"Here you go." The man across the counter handed her a huge plate of funnel cake covered in powdered sugar.

Gavin paid for the cake, and then ushered Emma over to an open spot on the field, where people were having pseudo-picnics. Kat wished she hadn't worn a dress, but she squatted down in the grass as best she could without flashing anyone.

Gavin seemed to notice her awkwardness, but as per usual, he said nothing. A man of very few words, really. She had no idea if he thought of her as just Emma's teacher or as a woman or if he even knew her name. When she'd first met him back in December, he'd looked at her like he'd wanted to know her name. But ever since, he'd barely spoken two words to her.

Emma sat between them, devouring the funnel cake. The young girl was one of her brightest students, but she was also painfully shy and had yet to make any friends her age. Kat felt for her: she'd been that way as a young girl. It wasn't until she'd reached adulthood that she'd begun to come out of her shell, although sometimes the shyness would return without warning.

Like now. Kat felt stupidly, obnoxiously shy around Gavin. She couldn't look at him, and she couldn't say anything beyond, "this is good" in reference to the funnel cake. And Gavin wasn't chatty, either, so they all sat there, silently eating the funnel cake like their lives depended on it.

But before long the cake disappeared, and Emma, restless and bored, jumped up to go collect flowers some yards away. Gavin told her not to wander too far, and he kept a careful eye on her as she gathered blue bachelor buttons and black-eyed Susans.

Kat was never like this around men. Men were easy. You smiled at them, you talked to them, you asked them questions about themselves. They in turn flirted with you, maybe touched you a little, and if things went well, you'd get a kiss and maybe a night's worth of fun. Kat had been single for over a year now since she'd come to Heron's Landing, and she'd felt the lack lately. But there was a dearth of eligible bachelors in these parts, so she'd gone without.

She gazed at Gavin as he watched Emma. He had dark hair like his brother, but he was a trifle shorter than Adam. He was broad in the shoulders and chest, and at the moment he sported a dark beard, which made him look a bit like a lumberjack. She knew he'd separated from his wife recently, but beyond that, he still remained a bit of a mystery.

His gaze caught hers, and she looked away.

Suddenly, a ball came soaring overhead, and someone shouted, "look out!" Before Kat realized what had happened, Gavin pushed her out of the way and they subsequently toppled onto the ground, and he ended up laying on top of her. He breathed hard as his chest pressed against hers, and she looked up into his eyes like a startled fawn.

"Are you all right?" he asked, his voice gruff.

She could only nod. She could make out tiny creases at the corners of his eyes, and there were a few glints of silver in his dark hair.

"There was a ball." He still looked at her, his elbows pressed to the ground beside her shoulders.

"So I gathered." She licked her dry lips.

His gaze zeroed in on her lips, and a thrill went through her. Was he going to kiss her? Right here?

He seemed to have an internal battle going on. He said something underneath his breath. Kat's eyes widened.

"Dad, what are you doing?"

He lurched upward, breaking the moment. She still lay on her back, staring up at the sky, as she listened to him say, "There was a ball. It almost hit Ms. Williamson."

She watched as he walked to stand over her, and he offered her his hand. She took it, and he pulled her up. He didn't let go of her hand right away. Looking like he was going to say something, she waited, her heart pounding.

But then Emma said, "Can we go get something to drink?"

Gavin let her go. "Sure." He looked at Kat. "Want to join us?"

Kat just shook her head and, mumbling about having to get somewhere, left the two of them to figure out what the hell that had all been about.

ABOUT THE AUTHOR

A coffee addict and cat lover, Iris Morland writes sexy and funny contemporary romances. If she's not reading or writing, she enjoys binging on Netflix shows and cooking something delicious.

irismorland.com